John Littlejohns

The Portent of Revolution

John Littlejohns

The Portent of Revolution

ISBN/EAN: 9783337236083

Printed in Europe, USA, Canada, Australia, Japan

Cover: Foto ©Andreas Hilbeck / pixelio.de

More available books at **www.hansebooks.com**

THE
Portent of Revolution.

BY

JOHN LITTLEJOHNS.

AUTHOR OF 'THE FLOWING TIDE.'
'ENGLAND AGAINST THE WORLD.'
'THE FROZEN NORTH.'

(*Translated into Russian.*)

ETC., ETC.

LAMPETER :
PRINTED BY THE WELSH CHURCH PRESS, LTD.
1899.

THIS BOOK

IS DEDICATED TO

MR. JAMES JEFFERY, PONTYPRIDD,

THE BEST

POLITICAL SCHOLAR IN WALES ;

WHOSE LIFE IS BOUND

UP WITH THE

PROCLAMATION OF TRUTH

IN ITS

ESPECIAL BEARING UPON THE

DESTINIES OF

NATIONS

PREFACE.

I have been impelled to write these observations upon the subject of Disestablishment by the extremely superficial way in which the question is being treated by the members and supporters of the Liberation Society. A careful perusal of the speeches dealing with the matter from the Radical standpoint together with a study of the Articles of the Liberationist press for a period of more than ten years has demonstrated to me that Disestablishment is intended to be secured by affirming that which the Liberationist is afraid to subject to the test of historical experience and Reason. The conclusions of our Nonconformist friends upon the question of Church and State always precede their premises with the result that hundreds of thousands of persons are being misled who have no time to devote to a consideration of the subject. I believe I am right in saying that Reason is never allowed to play its part in a Debate upon Disestablishment even by Radicals of parts and erudition who should scorn to hanker after a power that they believe can only be secured and retained by pandering to the prejudices of the people. If these pages should succeed in compelling the Liberationist to perceive that the Disestablishment of the Churches of England, Scotland, and Wales, *may be* fraught with gigantic issues to the future history of the world their object will have been achieved.

THE AUTHOR.

Ferndale, Nov. 28th, 1898.

THE CONTENTS.

THE

PORTENT OF REVOLUTION.

CHAPTER I

PURE REASON.

THE Rationalist tells us that we must believe nothing that we cannot substantiate by an appeal to the omnipotent powers of Reason. The formula is true, in so far as it does not encroach upon the domains of Faith. For it is certain that Reason and Faith are both required to comprehend the problems of Life and of human history. The capacity of the mind of man has, nevertheless, ever been a Theme for the exercise of the highest forms of thought and contemplation. Some philosophers have become so enthusiastic in their appreciation of its marvellous powers, that they have accredited it with potentialities that it was never intended to possess. Hence our patience has been sorely tried by the heritical ebullitions of Rationalism, of Positivism, and of the self denominated philosophies of history. We know that Reason is the highest attribute of intellectuality, but we also know that it is incapable of comprehending the strange questions that confront the enquiries of every age and country. Life is not its own custodian, and cannot, therefore, be the interpreter of its own decrees. The function of Reason is primarily to direct the propensities of conscience and to guide its bequests into channels of action. By its empressment we can both contemplate

[B]

things spiritual and material, and weigh all that can be said
or thought for or against them. Reason should therefore
be the mentor of agency in everything, the Ideality that
human effort should make the inspiration of its toils. Pure
Reason, in every age and clime, ought to be the centripetal
force for drawing the world away from its tendency to evil.
If employed for the objects for which it was created, it
would be productive of a type of conduct that would
personify our highest conceptions of Justice in the lives of
men. The privilege to think is the inalienable heritage
of rational beings, the obligation to think correctly the
forgotten duty of men. Life and death are subjected to
created material powers, but Thought can prevent itself
from being apprehended by any authority that the world
can command. What is Thought, and what are the limits
of its comprehensions? Every thought is the expressed
ratification of pure or impure Reason, every act is the
complement of a thought, the expression of the correct or
incorrect use of the highest faculty of the mind. Virtue
and vice may be said to be the materialized issues of the
approved or disapproved appeals which Reason has made to
behaviour and demeanour. Men are therefore entrusted
with a faculty that is capable of guiding their actions into
channels of perfection. The quintessence of Pure Reason
is Divinity incorporated into the potentiality of human
life, completeness designed to make the human race obedient to the revealed Will of God. The proper exercise of
the Faculty in past ages would have stamped the history
of the world with the approbation of immaculateness and
perfection. But as the Ideal has proved itself to be beyond
the reach of the real, so have the human records failed to
reach and to establish their pursuit of thoroughness and
maturity. Alas that man should have stumbled across his
own capacity, and have tarnished his life records with the
issues of his fall. His acts have been widely diversified, but
every act has ever been the progeniter of another promp-

ting. Thus have good and evil developed in men from their
root relationship to the perceptions of Pure Reason. In-
telligencies were intended to differentiate in degrees of
capacity, but no Intelligence has ever been sufficiently
enfeebled to be unproductive of thought and action. And
according to its diversifications, are we permitted to see the
results of its toil. So near might our conduct approximate
to perfection, that mental transmissions of sin would alone
separate it from its approximation to the life standards of
angels. But if pure Reason be not able to raise the mind
from its association with sin, it is at least able to prevent
this perversity of thought from expressing itself in deed.
Its application should be the parent of every labour and
industry. Its responses to our appeals should be the guide
of every deed. Is it right or is it wrong should be the pro-
genitive enquiry of every muniment and achievement.
Passion would be thus kept under control, prejudice prevented
from obscuring our perceptions of abstract right and wrong.
Deliberate acts are generally the results of the behests of
pure or impure Reason to a degree, spontaneous acts the
expression of our forgetfulness of its legislative capacity.
It is sometimes claimed that Imbeciles are the only persons
whose actions are unallied to Reason, but who will deny that
excitability frequently destroys Rationalism in persons whom
we know or believe to be sane. The human character
in its fallen state exhibits features that are antithetical, and
are therefore but half allied to Reason, as magnanimity and
pusillanimity, equability, and excitability, charity, and
greed, kindness and cruelty, self sacrifice, and selfishness,
blessing and cursing, the facility to maintain, and the
facility to destroy. But the conduct of a lunatic is not
always necessarily worse than that of a rational man.
Iniquity is a feature in the life of both, but the one
is spontaneous, whilst the other is a deliberate obscuration of the faculty of Reason. The spontaneous
ebullitions of the former can be anticipated and pro-

vided for, the designs of the latter manipulated so as to escape detection. Whatever the skill of imbeciles may be, it falls short of the determination to destroy Governments, and introduce anarchical eras, and of the necessity for foreseeing the possibility of being entrapped and discovered. A large proportion of the acts of Rational men are the results of an incapacity for balancing protuberating propensities by the exercise of the faculty of Reason. One of the chief objects of life should be the detection of flaws in our character, of mental projections that mar the judgment, and ally every conclusion to bias and partiality. Few are the individuals whose dispositions are pre-eminently the products of Reason by nature, fewer still those whose pertinacities are willing to be pounded into shape by the ironhammer of pure Reason. Voluptuousness, the most gratifying to the senses, is too frequently pursued with the foreknowledge that its issues must be fraught with evil. Present enjoyment destroys the memory of future retribution, and hands on its perversities of wickedness to succeeding generations of men. It is not denied that pure Reason was created to be the highest faculty of mental, moral, and material appeal, but the world's career is formed in contradistinction to its legislative enactments and judgments. Is the perversion of its powers to go on for ever? Will civilizations never rise sufficiently high to enforce its Decrees in the formation of individual and national character, and to compel them to coerce the passions that have hitherto produced the records of human history? Why were its coherencies not bequeathed to all types of created life, and why was the possibility of mental perversion reserved to man alone? Pure Reason was inspired to give him the custody of the world, and enable him to revel in a mental dominion that should transcend the bounds of Time, and open up the prospective glories of another world to come. It was created to act as the fulcrum for balancing the tendency of a will that was free to fall from the memorials of a life that had its beginning in time, but should have no ending in eternity. Had man availed himself of his inherencies of power, had he resolved to weigh every act in the scale of pure Reason, the history of the earth would have been resplendent, as dreamers have pictured it to be. Neither mental, moral, nor material delinquencies would have been allowed to cover the pages of history with their burning records of shame. The right to reflect and conclude would not have been interfered with by men who only possessed the powers of men, whose judgments they wished to subvert and to overcome. Diversities of conclusions would not have entrenched upon the dominion of thought, but would have acknowledged that their most brilliant inferences and deductions were still liable to be rejected by other men. Mental threats and demands would have been superceded by requests and desires, and by the acknowledgement that all human judgment was fallible, and likely to be wrong. The infliction of pain would have been arrested by the memory of the sorrow that pure Reason was created to destroy. The equity, which we only know as an abstraction, would then have encircled the brow of Life with the splendour of its Diadems. The bearing of one anothers burdens would have been transmuted from a high religious duty to the highest pleasure of life. We are not attempting to delineate the character of an uncreated race of beings, for all these possibilities are incorporated in the potentialities of the faculty of pure Reason. What is the foundation of the world's religious belief, but an attempt to accomplish by other means what individual man should always have accomplished for himself? What is the severest training of the human intellect, but the expressed determination to restore the mind to the tutelage of pure Reason? What are the classification of Society, and the pride of illustrious descent, but the efforts of nature to assist that determination by keeping its courses clear? What are the Sciences of mental and moral philosophy, but the codification of Reason's precepts for the attainment of such a noble end? The effort has succeeded to a degree, for culture now instructs its devotees to suppress every emotion that will momentarily or permanently affect the happiness of a fellow man. If pure Reason be the receptacle of Inspiration, and is inherent in human life, why have men hitherto failed to act up to its standard of exhilaration and cheer? History echoes back the question, and transmits it as a rich heritage to living men. The world's records have been forged by human obliquities, and turned to shame by the destruction of the Faculty of Reason. How few are the records of justice compared to the chronicles of iniquity and wrong! How spurned and scorned the mighty minds that have arisen to a sense of human potentiality, and to the need for diverting the courses of the world's career! How outnumbered are the glorious ages that have been blessed with the Socrates and Galileos, the Luthers and Newtons, the Burkes and Hugh Millars, and the other stars, who have asseverated the eternities of Truth that lie hidden in the archives of pure Reason! Alas, that the proclamations of the Faculty should be disdained to-day as shamefully as in the past, and that the age in which we live should be stamped with the world's of prejudice that are to subdue the perceptions of posterity. Alas, that the reservation of the discernment of Immortality to man should be the means of making him deny that there is a Life after Death. Our minds are either saturated with prejudice or with beliefs that admit of no investigation and enquiry. How long shall this iniquity continue? How long shall the exercise of less capable faculties be accepted as a recompense for the betrayal of the mighty talent that was created to rule the world? We turn from the contemplation of our responsibility with shame, but with no determination to arraign the soul of mental and moral oppression to the hell from which it should never have emerged. Prejudice will continue to be the criterion of our actions until another world's regime shall avert the mental freedom that we have debased. For Pure Reason has taken its final stand upon the maxim that with "what measure ye mete it shall be measured to you again."

Chapter II.

THE HUMAN WILL.

If Pure Reason is ever to assume its Province as the human arbiter of individual and national destinies it must be with the aid of the full powers of the human will. For the conception of a Truth is worthless unless we are prepared to abide at all hazards by its decrees. Physical courage is the pride and boast of all men, moral courage the pride and best of none. The weakness of the human will is either the primary or secondary cause of the downfall of human nature itself. Its feebleness is pitiable as a moral spectacle and replete with danger to the Principles that it was created to defend. Education is sufficiently powerful to strengthen certain elements of character, but it is impotent to raise the human will to an appreciation of its obligations and duties. Eighteen years of physical training turned the timid fellaheen of Egypt into heroes, and enabled them to bear the brunt of the Dervish attack at Omdurman, but a century of moral cultivation would not suffice to make them the adherents of virtue and Truth. Few are the men who know their own moral cowardice, fewer still those who venture to acknowledge and to overcome it. Myriads of human beings mistake stubbornness for Resolution, and pride themselves upon a great achievement when they have succeeded in defending some popular prejudice of the day. The characterisation of the human will is generally the crystallisation of stupidity moving in mental darkness and gloom. Human wills in their natural state resolve themselves into three classes, the effete, the stubborn and the normal. These will be found to correspond to the religious

perceptions of mankind, and to rise and fall according to
their moral values. Moral courage in its maturity is allied
either to genius or to the absorption of the principles of
Revelation, and is only displayed by the attachees of pure
Reason. The majority of human wills belong to the normal
class and protuberate from all phases of common character.
The possessors of them are ever the first to defend a
prejudice and to challenge its assailant to a combat in
which premises and conclusions, causes and effects are
heaped together in forms of inextricable confusion. These
men believe themselves to be the custodians of intelligence,
the preceptors of the mental activities of the soul.
Education has been absorbed into their carcases only
to develop their pusillanimous ideas, and to make
them the trundling products of pride, conceit, and
caste. Stubborn wills, however, belong to a species of
animalism whose propensities are ignorance of everything
in common and of culture in particular. Their weaknesses
can always be demonstrated by the expedient of demanding
that they pursue their will o' the wisps against the
opposition of Time. When tired out they prove themselves
to be assinegos in capability, propensity, and power. Effete
wills are possessed by persons of the lowest mental perception in the social scale. Their characteristics are either
recurring mental aberrations, kleptomaniacies, or a failure
to comprehend moral guilt apart from the degree of punishment that is meted out to it. Strong wills are as
unostentatious as they are rare, and are bent upon the
quiet pursuit of an object that will be far reaching in its
effect upon character. Their possessors are satisfied to be
pitted against the joint opposition of activity and of Time,
and are ever ready to decline a combat in which they are
certain to be the victors. As a mouse cannot arouse the
anger of the lion so cannot the shouts of a common crowd
rouse them to a sense either of approbation or of fear. The
majority of men will be found to belong to one or other of

the foregoing psychological classes under all conditions of life. So long as man refuses to defy the opposition of the world in matters of Truth, conviction, and enquiry, so long will pure Reason fail to raise the human race to a perception of its Ideal. And yet the human will cannot be nonproductive, cannot be dormantive, quiescent, or mentally dead. So long as blood circulates through the body so long will the untamed will run riot with thought, action, and exploit. It will fulfil the obligations of thought if requested to do so, it will lead the van of perception if left to its own resources. Satan may or may not find some mischief for idle hands to do, but it is certain that the mechanism of the human character will compel it to act intelligently or obstusely, purposeful or objectless, so long as life itself shall last. Time cannot hang listlessly around the transmissions of Intelligence for it is imperious in its resolve either to kill or to be destroyed. Our appreciation of volition is capable of an infinity of extremes, of expansions and contractions, of lifting the soul to heaven or of casting it down to hell. Its freedom is both its glory and its shame, its power to make and to undo character, its capacity to raise and to lower the records of human history. If it acts mechanically in its nadir of degradation and lifts the veil of eternity in its prescient zeal, it likewise endeavours to establish by implication that which it shrinks from proclaiming to be true. Inherited tradition soon becomes inherited prejudice and engages the human will to prevent itself from being analysed and attacked by the forces of Reason. Hence the blood that has besmeared the altar of human tyranny, the transmitted tendencies to perpetuate the iniquities of injustice and wrong. Hence the establishment of religions that have had their origin in the intellects of men, and that would be forced to annihilation if examined by the ethics of Reason. Hence the monuments of fraudulent trusts that we are asked to protect and to transmit to posterity. If the freedom of the human will were not sometimes reminded of its responsibilities by the Kingdoms of Providence and Grace, it would turn this world into a hell. If the resources of civilization can never be exhausted, neither will they ever desire of their own accord to cease from defending the prejudices of the fallen human will. Few are still the nations that will allow Reason to prosecute its appointed functions and decrees. The Rationalism that would make the world independent of God is only akin to the will that crushes will by the aid of material powers. How sepulchral must our boast of modern scientific achievements sound to constellations that know the trend of infinities together with their relationship to Reason and the human will. We are glad that some men have fought for the freedom of the human will, and established it in the councils of thought. We applaud Socrates as he drinks his cup of hemlock, Vigilantius as he scorns the wrath of the Vandals, Galileo as he smiles at the ignorance of the mighty council, Ridley and Latimer as they plunge into the fires that are to escort them into the sky, and Garibaldi as he spurns the accumulated hatreds of a fanatical foe. These are the men who have held aloft the heritage of the human mind, and defended the unity of Truth as the arbitrament of the world's order. The example that they have left behind will one day bear fruit in the encirclement of the human will with the power to perpetuate its decrees. Men will not always carry their prejudices to the grave, The majority will not constantly be accepted as types of the nations character, nor will their capacities be eternally subservient to the casualties of abandoned human wills. What are Poverty, ignorance, and crime but the reservations of nature's judgments for the abuse of her stern and unbending decrees? Would not the complete mastery of self by a single generation abolish them from the economies of the world? If the potentialities of the human will be so great, why have they not been utilized by the majority of men in the past? Is it because the mental strain necessary to the enforcement of their behests is too great for mortal man to bear? If so, by what overpowering faculty have they been crushed and overcome? If Pure Reason be the most competent mentor of life, and if the human will be the guardian queen of its decisions, why has the history of the world been produced in contradistinction to its manifestoes and precepts? Let the question be answered by the twelve hundred millions of living men who have sold their birthright to an abstraction and a miserable dream.

CHAPTER III.

ENVIRONMENT.

The faculties of Reason and the human will should have been the guardian queens of thought and action throughout the ages, but they have been allowed to lie dormant and dead as if allied to the world of dreams. The centuries are the inheritors of beliefs that have not been forged by the craftsmanship of equity, that have no place in the archives of Revelation, and that are fraught with increasing danger to the welfare of the world. The currents of history have been diverted from their appointed courses ; the Alpha and Omega of Time divided by a purpose of intrusion that was never their own. The heritage of the human race is largely a forgery whose Decretals are powerful to assuage the inhibitions of the mind, but whose issues are the touchstones of disease and death. Three quarters of the peoples of the globe are the jealous custodions of deception, the con-servators of energies that have subverted the functions of the intellect of man. The process of decay develops from age to age only to cover the virgin soil of Time with its infamies and decrees. We live in a vortex of prejudice, and have resolved to die amidst its billows too. Fanatics have arisen to sell their souls for power and to enslave generations that are still unborn. Infallibility is proclaimed by a council of men, and resolved into a creed by the destruction of the faculties of Faith and Reason. The influences of environment have become supreme in the art of forming character and of establishing creeds. Men are what their surroundings have made them. The phases of their lives are the reduplication of the phases of their encompassments, the accidents against which they have stumbled and fallen. Those who are born in savage countries become savages, those who enter civilised states become civilised men, those who make their appearance in places that partake of Savageries and Civilizations become the materialised products of both alike. As civilizations are appurtenances of degree, so are the characters of the men whom they produce appurtenances of degree also. Nature demands this result from the use that we have made of our faculties, and from the fact that mental coherencies are rarely controlled by the Kingdoms of Providence and Grace. Conduct, volition, and creed are alike the reproduction of the influences of environment. Truth and falsehood are generally proclaimed by the working of the same laws, and are dependent for success upon the same contributions of life. Revelation and mental creation will continue to run on the same track until a Fiat of eternity shall have robbed us of the mental freedom that we have debased. A man born in a Mohammedan country becomes a Mohammedan, a man born in a Confuscian state becomes a Confuscian, a man born in a Buddhist province becomes a Buddhist, a man born under the aegis of Christian influences becomes, in the majority of cases, a nominal Christian, and what is true of the whole is likewise true of its parts. A man born in Persia will be a hater of a fellow Mohammedan born in Turkey because his ancestors could not agree about the question of Prophetic succession. A man born in a Roman Catholic state will become a Roman Catholic. A man born in a Protestant country will become a nominal adherent of Protestantism. The exception to this proposition, as to every other thing, only proves the rule. Froude very properly reminds us that whether we regard Christianity as a miracle from without, or as developed from within, out of the conscience and intellect of man we perceive, at any rate, that it grew by natural causes, that it commended itself by argument and example, that it was received or rejected according to the moral and mental condition of those to whom it was addressed. The public questions of the nineteenth century must be settled upon a recognition of the facts of history. Faith may outstrip its functions and make requests to the Almighty that Reason itself was created to grant, but its cries will not be heeded in Heaven. Revelation and experience must be allied for the better government of the world. The talents of men must continue to co-operate with Faith and Providence until the advent of the millenium. We need not, however, despair. Falsehood will not be allowed to race upon terms of equality with Truth for ever. The possession of the faculties of the human mind will one day be arrested by the Hand of a Dictatorship, before whose mandates solar systems will pass away. The noblest of intellects will not always be tortured by their own enquiries or be allowed to pine for some manifestation of Divine authority in the counsels of the world. We shall not be under a perpetual obligation to surmount the facts of existence, or to frame our courses as if man was the sole arbiter of this grand old globe's career. Let Reason and Faith issue their proclamations a little longer and the human intellect will be freed from the portentous responsibilities that have borne it to the ground. That Christianity is a Revelation is evidenced by the continuation of identical Jewish life, but it is nevertheless true that it is allied to common sense to a far greater degree than is any other Religion in the world. It does not spurn the laws of evidence so far as its credentials are concerned, but it claims to be not of this world in respect of the deducements that be beyond the ken and grasp of human reason. If its Divinity were established by miraculous interference with the laws of nature the faculties of the human mind would by such an act be rendered null and void. We must evolve the freedom of the world by the concentration and adaptation of all the talents that we possess, for not until these

have fought and lost the battle can common sense demand
that Eternity shall interfere. Every generation has to play
a conscious or an unconscious part in the human drama;
every age must lead the world nearer or further away
from God. It was the perception of this fact that caused
the ancient Greeks to formulate their thoughts under the
various classifications of Philosophy, and to hand them
down to the generations who were still to come. What is
true of national idiosyncrasies and creeds is also true
of individual characteristics dispositions and castes.
Environment has subverted the functions of Reason in all
ages and countries. National conceptions of justice and
morality are but the conformations of its decrees, whilst
individual propensities are the materializations of the very
air that they breathe. The muniments of society are but
the incorporated appointments of dead men, the criminal
instincts of the lowest social orders but the reincarnations of
the prejudices of the grave. And what is true of the extremes
of society is likewise true of the whole of its parts. The child
is father to the man only because the man will not avail himself of his talents to rid himself of the prepossessions of the
child. If the nursery atmosphere be saturated with atheism
and lies, the children will become atheists and liars in their
turn. If the parents be evil livers the children will be
evil livers until circumstances compel them to change their
environment. If the family escutcheon has not been
tarnished for centuries, it will not be tarnished for centuries
to come. When nations and individuals appear to rebel
against their environment they direct their efforts against
its more galling burdens, and not against the influences of
environment itself. The new environment will have the
same power as the old, and will affect character in the same
way. Thus has no nation ever been known to rebel against
a national religion that affected their minds, whilst leaving
their bodies alone. A great mind may sometimes arise to
destroy an environment that he believes to be inimical to

the interests of the people whose character it has formed,
but the successes with which he has temporarily awakened
the wills of men to a sense of their servitude will be but
co-existent with his own life. The new enironment will
work upon the same bases as the old. Luther may rise
superior to his surroundings to destroy the Catholicism of
Germany, but succeeding generations of his countrymen
will not generally be able to say why the Pope's religion
has been superceded by a purer faith. The influences of
environment are never questioned with regard to others,
but are indignantly challenged when applied to ourselves.
It may almost be safely said that the Thought can only be
specifically endowed with a perception of its powers by the
occasional affront that alone will draw out a part of its
resources. There are an environment of body, and an
environment of mind. Correct deportment is more the
product of accident than· of Reason. Orthodox beliefs
are held and defended by men who have never questioned
their titles to honour. The Scions of noble families frequently conform to Truth, because their patrimonies would
be forfeited by the surrender of it. Better that Truth
shall be thus defended than abandoned, better that conduct
shall be mechanically correct than that it shall be wrong.
The life of man is chiefly a life of accident, because of the
transmitted tendency to subordinate mental toil to the
acquisition of peace and ease. We shrink from the labour
of thought, because it implies a strain that the human will
is too weak to bear. Original thinkers form but a small
proportion of the worlds inhabitants, and few ever of these
bring their theoretic conceptions to the practises of life.
The thunders of Spinoza, of Comte, and of Spencer, are but
stage mechanisms, and are outclassed as values by the
martial strains of Atbara and Omdurman. Historians fire
the world with their depictions of human tyranny, but leave
the work of Reform to other hands. And what is true of
conduct, is particularly true of religious belief. Few men

[c]

believe ought save what their fathers believed before them. Truth and falsehood are handed on by the same laws, and expanded or contracted according to the degree of applied material power amongst which they obtain. They can be gauged by their willingness or unwillingness to submit themselves to an examination by the faculties of the human mind, and by their appeal to the higher faculty of Faith. Neither can the postulate be questioned because Christianity differentiates between a nominal and an incarnated profession of Truth. The assertion is both true as applied to religious belief itself and as applied to the subdivisions of creed. The Turks and Persians both adhere to the faith of Mohammed, as aforesaid, but hate each other because their respective ancestries could not agree about the appointment of the Prophet's successor. Dervishes will continue to torture themselves so long as the custom is allowed to survive. The Juggernaut will not pine for victims until its wheels shall have ceased to revolve. The Hindoo will continue to make caste an object of worship and of fear until the voice of Reason shall have called the sword of Christendom to strike his fanaticism down. The Spaniard will only learn that there is no visible body on the face of this material globe to whose decrees men must submit in the matter of private judgment, when his mental slavery shall have been destroyed by the avenging armies of pure Reason. But even those whose faculties have been trained to examine every proposition upon its merits, are frequently the slaves of a form of environment. Is the law of love fulfilled in the the lives of its professors, and do they treat their enemies as if they were their friends? Is Revenge less sweet to them than to devotees of baser creeds, and are they satisfied to let the spirit of Retaliation rest in its grave. It is said that the nineteenth century of the Christian era is the most accomplished of the centuries of time. We are told that Gibbon was wrong when he declared that if a man were called upon to fix the period in the history of the world during which the condition of the human race was most happy and prosperous, he would, without hesitation, name that which elapsed from the death of Domition to the accession of Commodus. If the declarations of scientists be correct our age should be free from the prejudices that have tarnished the thought of other ages, and from the possibility of living under a wrong belief by the operations of environment. But is it so? Look at our schools of thought and see whether it is not true that the wildest theories have but to be publicly proclaimed to be believed. A popular Statesman turns his back upon the cardinal principles that he has professed for more than sixty years, and hundreds of his followers not only applaud his tergiversations, but endeavour to make us believe that he never held contrary opinions at all. Our Universities were organized to impart systems of knowledge that should always be open to attack by the batteries of Reason, but what are the majority of the men whom they turn out but benefactors of the prejudices that obtain within their walls. Crowds of graduates would only think of questioning the Truth of their Tutors' opinions when the Tutors happen to be minors in the academic scale. The same characteristics are exhibited by all educated men, and frequently to a greater degree. They adopt the opinions of their Authors with unconscious alacrity, and trot them out as their own under every form and phase of discussion. The majority of academicians are only trained animals turned adrift to propagate the prejudices of their several schools. The Undergraduates who came under Newman's influences, never could remember that he was only a fallible man. Narrow and intolerant colleges will continue to produce narrow and intolerant men. The Spaniards and Swedes will continue to be the products of their surroundings so long as the present mental regime shall endure. The former are everywhere bigoted and cruel, the latter, as naturally cultured, affable and kind. No trained animals before the footlights ever exhibited the influences of environment better than the nations referred to. As it is with systems, so is it with the social traditions of society. Rich men proceed almost instinctively to Yale and Oxford, intellectual men as instinctively to Harvard and Cambridge. Nonconformity is bitterly opposed to agnosticism and atheism, yet a transmitted prejudice has caused its adherents to work for a common political object with its foes. The proclamations of mental iaptitude have burned their fires into our lives, and have cast us into the arms of the portent of Revolution.

CHAPTER IV

HOW MEN AND NATIONS HAVE RECEIVED THE TRUTH AND HAVE LOST IT AGAIN.

Human history is generally the record of man's attempt to subvert the eternal purposes of God. Those purposes were conceived before Creation was begun, and they will last when Time shall be no more. The deep echoes of eternity proclaimed that worlds should be suspended upon pillars of light to become the custodians of an Incarnation of Thought that was to typify the higher life of man. Majestic as was the spectacular expansion of atoms unto worlds, the effulgency of reflected thought was more resplendent still. The exercise of its capacities would enable man to soar above the attributes of Angels, and to encompass the career of a world that was bequeathed to their care with enduring monuments of its destinies. Human thought could surround the human zone with the highest objects of its ambition, and could begird its resolves with Ideas that should transcend the limits of Death. The expression of desire was to become the parent of action, the morning star that should demonstrate to the world the trend of Immortality. The human Intellect was formed to portray the consciousness of a Life that should become the guardian queen of the graces of eternity. Reason might torment the questionings of Faith in Time, but its enquiries would certainly be superbly answered in the world to come. The soul is a fire that can burn the portents of its destinies into the why and wherefore of our being, and lead us on to an appreciation of the enternal purposes of God. Men and nations may come and go, but those purposes will go on for ever. Human systems may rise and fall, but the purposes of Creation will not heed the echoes of their exhilarations and despairs. Aeons of freedom may be succeeded by ages of tyranny, but the first great cause will move towards its goal amid the blessings and cursings of their advancements and ruins. Civilizations and barbarisms may struggle for the supremacy—their ashes will but kindle into new forms of Life the everlasting purposes of Heaven. Human history proclaims in fiery lines that the triumphs of wrong shall not go on for ever. Nations' destinies shall not always appear to be the fortunes of chance, or the arbitraments of artificial supremacy. It was decreed before the first chapter of the human annals was penned, that the greatness of the world's empires should be subservient to the objects of their careers. Napoleon conceived Providence to be on the side of the big battalions, but the thunders of Waterloo awakened him from his reverie, as they demanded a just recompense for the fires of death that he had kindled in the world. England and not France was destined to become the modern human arbiter of the world's career. We return the cynical smile that confronts our insular prejudices as we point to the Empire jewels that blaze amid the dazzling lights of the British Crown. It was not chance that enabled a lieutenant from Aden to forestall a French fleet by a few hours in hoisting the English flag on Perim. It was not fortune that enabled Bass and Flinders with a boat's crew to secure Tasmania to England by arriving there just before Bougainville's great French expedition made its appearance. It was not Fate that enabled Governor Phillips with his convicts to save Australia to England by hoisting the English flag at Port Jackson two days before La Perouse came within view of the place. History is full of eccentricities that Philosophy cannot explain, and that have no connection with the idiosyncrasies of Fate. Men and nations have perceived the true purposes of Life and have lost them again, and men and nations are still entangled in the meshes of the same unperceived enquiries. The perception of the eternal purposes was lost by Adam even after he had received it directly from God. The family of Abraham lost it after the Promises had been repeatedly made and reserved to himself and his children. The nation of the Jews lost it when reconnoitring the fact that their history was a splendidly sustained miracle. And their forgetfulness was destined to affect the fortunes of human history as they had never been affected before. It was immortalized by the Divine refusal to allow them to drive out all the nations from Canaan, and by the transposition of those nations into instruments of punishment and death. It was subdued majestically by the captivities and by the foundation of the succession of mighty Empires that were to be requisitioned to carry out their more terrible developments in the future. The Advent of the Messiah was timed by its deathless memories, and attached by the final rejection of his claims to the mighty scenes that were to end in the dispersion of the Jews throughout the countries of the globe. The thunders of the commands of Titus and Hadrian still break upon our ears as they portend the Revolution that was set in so many centuries of Jewish blood. Rome fell when its work was done, whilst out of its ruins have been carved the national preponderancies that are now seen to have synchronized with the perception of the everlasting purposes of God. The processes of devolution are still going on; Empires are rising and falling like stars that measure the orbits of the Eternities. But Rhetorical effects are not the objects that we wish to achieve. Generalizations carry no weight when unsupported and allowed to rest alone upon their merits. The records of Jewish apostasy by the powers of environment have a grand bearing upon the political policies of the age in which we live. So enfeebled did the Jews become, as the result of their sojourn in the land of the Pharaohs, that they could with difficulty first remember what Moses meant by the God of their fathers. They knew the meaning of idolatry only too well in the abstract, but they could not summon the will power that was necessary to obscure the material and sensible Images by which they were surrounded. They fell into idolatry whilst their Leader was temporarily absent receiving the sacred ordinances from the hand of God. Joshua perceived that environment would frustrate his purposes if once his followers rested before the remnant was driven out of the land. And after Joshua there arose another generation which knew not Jehovah, nor yet the works which He had done for Israel. The worship of Baal begun to be practised, and the idols of the country to become the objects of Jewish veneration. The apostates were given into the hands of enemies whose gods they had made their own. The worship of Baal was soon publicly practised, and the people did not scruple to avow their readiness to display their zeal for the object of their love. Even David, whose life and history, says Carlyle, are the truest emblem ever given us of a man's moral progress and welfare here below, allowed his Reason to be repeatedly overthrown by the influences of his surroundings. Achish, the Philistine, put such confidence in the captured David, that he summoned him to join in a grand attack which the Philistines were preparing against Israel, *and David sank so low as to boast of the courage he would display.* Nor was Solomon sufficiently wise to maintain his Faith against the attacks of environment. The law of ritribution for sinful acts by their natural effects, we are told, worked in him from the very first, and the wise man married an Egyptian woman only to become a participant in her idolatry. Rehoboam likewise demonstrated the tendencies of environment, for the luxury in which he was trained gave him a headstrong character in which his fathers precepts were soon thrown away. Both he and his people declined into idolatry and practised the most abominable vices of the nations around. Jeroboam also fell to become the creature and creation of his surroundings. He resorted to the idolatry which he had witnessed in Egypt, and likened his Maker to a grazed ox. Omri founded a dynasty in Samaria, which surpassed all that had gone before it in wickedness, so that his statutes became a byeword for a course that was opposed to the law of Jehovah. Ahab was purely the slave of his environment for he established the worship of Baal throughout Israel, and brought on the darkest night of Israel's spiritual declension. Elijah was compelled to slay the Priests of Baal because they were apostate Israelites who had forgotten the Law, and had brought themselves under the penalties against idolatry. Jehoram first of all put down the worship of Baal, but when he married Athaliah, the daughter of Ahab and Jezebel, he soon imbibed the idolatrous spirit of that evil house. Ahaz, the twelfth King of Judah, likewise plunged into all the idolatries of the surrounding nations, made molten images for Baal, sacrificed his children to Moloch in the Valley of Hinnom, and offered sacrifices in the high places, one on every green hill and under every green tree. Manasseh's idolatries included every form of false religion and abominable vice that Israel had ever learnt from the heathen nations. The captivities may be truthfully said to have been occasioned by the necessity for destroying the influences of environment. We are, nevertheless, enabled to cite Isaiah, Jeremiah, Ezekiel, and Daniel as examples of those who stood firm against its awful encroachments and powers. When Ezra applied himself to the work of Reformation, says a distinguished writer, he found the people already infected with the evil that had proved the root of all the former mischief, inter-marriage with the idolatrous nations around them. The sins of the Jewish nation henceforth took a direction altogether different from the open rebellion and apostacy of their fathers, but they were still subservient to the formative influences of character. The more scrupulous their observance of the law, the more did they make it void by their traditions, and subversive of all that was noble and good. When Herod appeared upon the scene the sacred name had almost disappeared from the Jewish recollection, but it was resumed for the Idumaen usurper to reunite the nation, to heathenize its government, and to prove the need and smooth the way for the advent of the Messiah. The holy hill, to which David had carried the ark of God, was allowed to look down upon a theatre and amphitheatre, in which Herod held games in honour of Augustus, musical and dramatic contests, horse and chariot races, together with the bloody fights of gladiators and wild beasts. The eternal purposes seemed to have been forgotten by the Israelites, but they were destined to blaze forth in a new triumph by the departure of the sceptre from Judah. The effort to maintain a guardianship of the Truth proved too much for the Jews, as it has since proved too much for some of the nations who have succeeded to the heritage that they fain would have destroyed. 'Will ye also go away,' asked the Messiah of the Disciples as He perceived the over bearing attitude of environment upon the assem ly before Him. 'Though all men should be offended yet will not I,' was an impulsive declaration that soon developed into the denials, imprecations, and curses that shewed the weakness of the speaker's will. 'Demas hath forsaken me,' said St. Paul because he hath loved this present world.' The same environing propensities that estranged the enthusiastic Demas from the paths of Pure Reason afterwards captivated, estranged, and heresied a large part of the early Church. The sad truth, says an ecclesiastical historian, is that as soon as Christianity was generally diffused, it began to absorb corruptions from all the lands in which it was planted, and to neglect the complexion of all their systems of religion and philosophy. The philosophy and vain deceit, according to the traditions of men, by which some had begun to spoil the Church of Colossae, were of the same kind as the profane and vain babblings, and opposition of Knowledge falsely so called, from which Timothy was urged to turn away. Corruption crept in because environment not be kept out. St. John knew the power of it when he determined to refuse the heretics even the intercourse of social life. In our age the sweet and saintly Keble followed his example to remain sitting in the porch of a house at which he intended to call, because a heretical member of the family unexpectedly happened to be at home. But the subjugation of the Jews and of large numbers of the early Christians by the powers of environment has also been succeeded by the failure of Christian states to maintain even the semblances of Christianity. It is of supreme impor tance to a correct perception of the trend of contemporary events that we should understand that the majority of the Mohammedan countries of to-day were once professors of the Christian Faith. The laws of nature are uniform throughout the world, and are unconscious of changes in the conditions and ages of human life. Like causes will continue to produce like effects so long as Time itself shall last. What a contrast do northern Africa, Asia Minor, and Eastern Europe now present to the mighty records of their past. Where are now the Apologists of Tertullian, Cyprian, Augustine, Athanasius, Basil, and Chrysostom? Are they to be found in the lands that gave these Christian Fathers birth? What has become of the countries in which they laboured, and why do they no longer add recruits to the noble army of martyrs? History affirms in her most impressive tones that a change of environment produced a change of Faith, amongst the peoples whom they taught and loved. Persia, Arabia, Egypt, Abyssinia, Northern Africa, Turkey, Asia Minor, all lend semblance to the great truth that the majority of men and nations will become the products of their surroundings so long as the human will shall continue to be free. The early Christians of Persia are known to have sustained a glorious thirty years persecution and to have cheerfully died for the Faith. Their enervated and enfeebled and debiliterated successors, however, paid a tribute of two million pieces of gold to Islam as the price of their fidelity and their shame. Baneful would be the memories of their treachery if we belonged to a different species and were influenced by different natural laws. Did the sage who beheld the primitive lustre of St. Sophia at Constantinople, and who enumerated its colours, shades, jaspers, and porphyries, its balustrade of the choir, its capitals and pillars, its 40,000 pounds weight of silver, and its holy vases of pure gold enriched with inestimable gems, believe that the day was coming when that Queen of Churches would despise the shame of the Cross! Do the people of to-day reflect that their political acts will be re-incarnated in history, perhaps to denounce the intentions that gave them birth? The atmosphere is surcharged with laws that take no rest and that victimize the actions of Civilizations and Barbarians alike. Modern Kingdoms are moving heedlessly along and are establishing and perpetuating principles whose issues they neither foresee, nor understand. Proofs of the continuity of like historic results can be seen in the maintenance of national prejudices to-day. One is tempted to smile at the superficial attempts that have been made to quash the cause of Ireland's recurring hatreds and discontents. Irish character cannot be changed so long as it continues to be produced by its present environment. If Ireland's religious conceptions are right, she would be false to truth, if she submitted to the supremacy of England. She is justified by the covenants of her creed in concentrating all her energies for the overthrow of Anglo-Saxon heretical power, and establishing herself in an alliance with some nation, that has not rejected what she believes to be the Will of God. Why did Ireland reject the Protestant Reformation when it had been accepted by England, Scotland, and Wales? Was it because Ireland's perception of Truth was more brilliant than that of the Sister Kingdoms? If so would not the Kingdoms of Providence and Grace have compelled Great Britain to submit to the Dictatorship of the Emerald Isle, and to assist Ireland in making its

creed that of the larger British Empire? We believe that
Ireland was not converted to Protestanism, *because Irishmen
were appealed to in a language that they did not understand.*
The Reformation was accepted by the Bishops of Meath,
Limerick, and Kildare, but rejected again because the rude
Kerne's of Ireland overpowered the appeals that had been
made to Ireland's Reason, and to the intellectualities of
Irish individual and national life. Had Archbishop
Browne's promise to translate the Reformed Liturgy
into Irish been fulfilled, Ireland would have become
a Protestant nation, and not the product of the
Catholicism that we know her to be to-day. Why did
Belgium, France, and Spain respond to the appeals
that were made to their Reasons, and then again surrender
their thinking powers to the ecclesiastical castes that had
for so many centuries, kept them under control? Common
sense answers that they followed the varying fortunes of
their environment and submitted to the influences that
succeeded in the end. The religious beliefs of the three
countries followed the swing of the national pendulum and
found their resting places where and when it ceased to
move. The inquisition, and the massacre of St. Bartholomew,
failed to shake the Reformed Faith, so long as it was supported by surrounding public opinion, but when the latter
was changed as the result of overpowering political acts and
the old environment re-established, France, Belgium, and
Spain became Roman Catholic countries once more. Few
living Spaniards are aware that thirty-two thousand of their
ancestors were burned to death in Spain, because they tried
to change the religious beliefs of the State that had given
them birth. Few contemporary Frenchmen are aware that
France was once equally divided in creed, and that the
zealots of the surviving belief had to resort to subterfuge
and political acts to establish their Faith upon the ruins of
that of the foe. When Alciat filled the chair of Law at
Bruges, Calvin found the popularity of the Reformed Doc-

trines oppressive to his own wave of repose. 'By nature somewhat clannish,' says he, 'I always sought the shade and ease, and would have preferred some hiding place : but this was not permitted, for all my retreats became like public schools.' What a flood of memories does the Revocation of the edict of Nantes bring to the thoughtful mind, and how well does it remind it of the fact that political acts can change a nation's religious belief and character. We smile as we admit that this may be abstractedly true but cannot be allowed to apply to the prejudices that we ourselves have conceived, and that we mean to establish and to defend. Our vanity must be fed even when it falsely avows that opportunism cannot endanger the results that nature has transfixed to certain current causes. The orator who appeals to our passions will continue to be rewarded with the most flattering unctions of our applause. Let the dicta of history be to the wiseacres who are dull enough to peer into the future, they must not be allowed to interfere with our contempt of singularity and the pleasantry that follows in its wake. But we must proceed to demonstrate that not only have nations grasped the truth and lost it again, but that the processes of mental operation have victimized the majority of individuals who have come under a differentiating environment. We all know the story of the convict who resolved to maintain his reason by the simple act of throwing pins about his cell and finding them again. Contemptible as such a reference may be judged to be by the political jugglers of the day, it nevertheless proves that environment is almost absolute in its effects upon character. And is not the inference well substantiated by the case of the Prussian Newfeld, who was rescued from a living death in the Dervish Prison at Khartoum after the battle of Omdurman. Were not Newfeld's reason and memory affected by his long captivity, and had he not become the materialized product of his surroundings? Was he not a Christian when he entered the prison, and a Mahommedan when he came out

of it again ? Could the stream of tendency be expected to
let him alone, when its mission was to try the strength of
the world's Reason and will ? Has it ever left the majority
of Englishmen and Americans alone, when travelling in
foreign countries, and when it needs the exercise of a super-
human effort to rise above the environment that affects
them through the eye ? Every travelled man knows that
temperament everywhere succumbs—with the exception of
the miraculous maintenance of the character of the Jews—
to the material influences of its surroundings. Englishmen
attend Sunday Bullfights in Spain, Sunday races in France,
and Sunday plays at the theatres of Vienna, and Bucharest,
and San Francisco. The ecclesiastical æsthetic forgets his
reckoning at sea and joins his fellow travellers to the
ordinary dinner on Friday. Interesting as the world is to
the spirit of contemplation, it is more interesting to the
student who watches its effects upon prejudice and
character. Truth and falsehood are promoted by the operations of the same laws, and establish themselves by the
agencies of the same kinds of enterprise. The lives and
beliefs of men and nations are what their surrounding have
made them. God's will is both remembered and forgotten
by the strength or weakness of the forces that flaunt it in
the faces of men. No generation labours so much for itself
as for posterity, because its sensible corporate action does
not begin until half its life has gone. What therefore is to
be the measure of our contribution to the future ages of the
world ? Are we going to hand on the issues of great questions that we have not the strength of will to decide for
ourselves and for our children ? Or are we going to allow
the grand emanations of Time to be obscured and thwarted
by the influences of prejudice and the accidents of environment ? Are we prepared to authorize brazen faced Demago-
gues to dilate upon subjects that their mental powers are
too feeble to understand, to inflame passions that even men
of capacity cannot control, to declaim against historic systems

that are beyond the ken of their little grasps, and that can only be assailed at the cost of arresting the real evolutions of the world's history? Is the age to be given up to charlatans and political mountebanks, and to the puny pretenders who are prepared to float to power upon the stream of human tendency? How long are these quacks to be permitted to insult the aureoles of human Reason with their empiricisms and opportunisms, their puerilities and surfeits of monkeyisms, their dawdling mimicries of sentiment and conviction, and the brutalized satires and coarse ironies with which they assail the perceptions and tastes of intellectual men? Have our visions become so darkened that we cannot see the trend of contemporary events, the issues of current policies in the larger life of the world? We stand on the brink of Time to play our part in the evolution of human history! Shall we be cursed or applauded for our mental and material transmissions to posterity? The memories of our age will either be enshrined in garlands of grateful recollection, or maledicted and anathematized for our obscuration of the trend and purport of the higher counsels of the world.

CHAPTER V

THE CAUSE OF ENGLAND'S GREATNESS.

The obligation to discuss the problems of individual and national life is acknowledged by all schools of thought with the reservation that every deduction must be hypothetical and inapplicable to the burning questions of the day. Environment has so stamped our prejudices into the tissues of our beings that no power on earth is strong enough to eradicate its imports from our minds. The brows of some of the best reasoners of the day become darkened when compelled to confess that their pre lilections are palpably wrong. Bias controls the sequence of thought both in respect of the lives of individuals and of nations. We see it in the *vox populi* of the age, and in the special pleading of the social and political partizans of the world to-day. What could more systematically demonstrate the powers of environment than the mob law of America, or the madness that characterizes the conduct of public political meetings in the Emerald Isle. We know that our lives ought to be devoted to the discovery and application of Truth, but we forget the fact as soon as we leave our studies to mingle with our fellow-men. We are aware that our social and political enquires should be deep and conscientious, but we are too weak to act up to the spirit of the dictum. We are conscious that our predilections may be the very antithesis of Truth, but we apologize for the conviction when confronted by the materializations of sincerity. We cannot contend against the gibes of fools, because they are the elements of the environing powers that expose the weak-

[D]

nesses of our wills. Civilization has done muc to improve the world, but it has failed to touch the influence of environment upon our lives. Is it therefore of any avail to plead for the supremacy of human Reason in the consideration of the policies of the day? Is it of any utility to remind our fellow-men that prejudice should not be transmitted to our children, and that Faith should not be requisitioned to conceive problems that do not lie beyond the ken and grasp of Reason? The affirmations of material results should not be permitted unless these results are ready to put themselves into the crucible of rational examination, and subject themselves to the ordinary laws of evidence. Life is a great mystery, but it can never be made more mysterious by the word of its own species. The world is impregnated both with the causes of its own condition, and with remedies that are capable of changing its character. Revelation and imposture have both been adopted as standards of Life, and have only been prevented from becoming omnipotent by the Providence that rules the world. The martyrdoms of good men have not been more physically courageous than the fanatical self-abnegations of bad men, and have not more influenced the laws under which our characters are formed. What then are the positions of living nations in the scale of the world? What are the relative powers and influences of Buddist, Confuscian, Mohammedan, and Christian Kingdoms and States at the present time. Why do disparities subsist, if they subsist at all? Why are not all nations equal, since they belong to a common type of Life? The question is both answered by Revelation and by the experience of human history. The quarter-master may steer the ship, but the course most be marked out for him by the master of the vessel. Empires rise and fall according to their perception of the influences that form character, and of the arbitrament of character upon the destinies of the world. As Christendom has brought into subject in the other parts and nations of the globe, so has England become the most influential power of Christendom. Is this the result of accident as our atheistic fellow-citizens are so fond of telling us? If so, is it not strange that the accident should not have produced contrary results and have established the nations that have made present licentious happiness their chief object in life? Is it not incomprehensible that the accident should have produced the same results as what Revelation has taught us to expect? If our Empires supremacy is but the consequence of accident what hope can we have of its continuance for another single day? If accident be the cause of our national greatness and the producer of the eighty-four per cent of battles that we have won in the course of our history, can we rely upon its stability for success in the future? Were Marlborough, Wolfe, Clive, Nelson, and Wellington believers in the theory of accident would not its uncertainties have made them afraid to meet more powerful foes than themselves? Can the belief in accident be substantiated as a canon of Logic and impressed upon the mind of anyone who attempts to trace the connection between cause and effect? England's Religion may be laughed to scorn because it is out-of-date, but we ask again why has England's material power been allowed to be retained by a country that is fossilized and bigoted and ecclesiastically wrong? It is a fact—whether based upon accident or not—that the powers of living nations correspond to their perceptions of Truth, Reason, Justice, and of what they have deduced to be the revealed will of God. The ratio of material power to geographical areas and to population has been reversed, and England has become the mistress of three of the five Continents of the world. Our object, however, is not to argue with the Atheist so much as with a school of thinkers, whose Logic is lopsided and whose false conclusions are making themselves the most dangerous enemies whom England has had to confront. If national greatness be the outcome of character, we are compelled to look for the differentiating propensities between our own country and other nations. If no such differences exist, the doctrines of the Atheist may, for all that we can demonstrate to the contrary, be true; but if such disagreements obtain we naturally ask whether they appertain to what we believe to be Revelation or not. England is a Christian country, but so is France as far as a nominal profession of faith is concerned. Wherein then lies the difference between Britain and the Gallic State? The difference is to be found in the taunt that we take our pleasures sadly. England is said by her enemies to have surpassed the nominal religious professions which are sufficient for them and to have incorporated her Faith into her character. She adheres to academic Christian disquisitions when she perceives that they have no practical bearing upon life, but she enforces their decrees when she assumes that they were intended to produce character. She does not claim to make men religious by national establishments because the results to be obtained are known to be immaterial ones, but she does aspire to influence them by making the environment of the country the Imagery of the embodied Faith. This is both the secret of her success and the glory of the sensibility with which she acknowledges Christianity to be not of this world, and yet compels it to give unto Caesar the things that are his. This is her fierce insight into the obligations attaching to the Commandments; her apprehension of the fact that they can only be entirely corporeally obeyed by the Union of Church and State. The foresight and insight of the English and Scottish Reformers three hundred and fifty years ago was the corner stone of a mighty Empire's greatness. The transmission of their prescience into the defence of the unity of created social powers and into the spirit of the country's Legislation was to be rewarded by the dissemination of British influences throughout the countries of the globe. As England is the only country that has perceived the import of the Commandments, and the fact that they cannot be fully obeyed without the Union of Church and State, so is she the only country that has been permitted to civilize and to Christianize the major portion of the globe. Let those who assail our national position tell us whether the State was created for any purpose at all, and whether its preponderating influences were given it to be used as an attack upon the Revealed Faith or not. Was the Creator of the Church not also the Creator of the State, and did he form the latter for no purpose whatsoever? Or, if the State was destined to be degraded to ignoble purposes, was it not forseen that it would cause weak human wills to become the servers of its omnipotent decrees? Could the early Church withstand its degrading influences without the miraculous intervention of Heaven? Is there a nation living that holds a different religious belief to that of the Statute Book by which it is governed? Will like causes cease to produce like effects so long as time itself shall last? Had the Reformers answered these questions differently to what we know them to have done, would the British nation have attained to the proud position that it holds to-day? A negative answer is supplied to the question by the position of the countries that have refused to follow England's example, and that have been given as a consequence inferior places amongst the created forces of the world. 'Although the Law given from God by Moses as touching Ceremonies and Rites do not bind Christian men, nor the civil precepts thereof ought of necessity to be received in any Commonwealth, yet, notwithstanding, no Christian man whatsoever is free from the Commandments, which are called moral.' The quotation will be found in the Articles of the National Church of our country. How beautifully do they bear out the results that we have been taught to seek in the archives of experience and in the Book of Revelation. The germs of Imperialism that are the inheritances of the Anglo-Saxon race ignominiously failed to establish an Empire until the

Reformers' creeds subverted the social economies and made them subservient to the formation of Christian character. So long as our national Ideal was no higher than that of the Continent of Europe, so long were the military victories of England barren of material result. What are Cresy, Poictiers, and Agincourt but preceptors of Blenheim, Plassy, and Waterloo without their moral values? It was reserved for the Reformers to establish a deep insight into the purposes of Revelation and existencies of Power, to unite them for the attainment of the highest objects of life, and to produce a national character that, with many failings and faults, should still be obedient to the reaveled will of God. The effects of their prescience are perceived long after their causes have been consigned to forgetfulness and oblivion. The Reformers' fidelity has been acknowledged in the creation of the influences that England has cast around the shadows of the world, and in the creation of the most resplendent captivations of Imagery that ever blazed their jewels from Aureole or Kingly crown. Human history is not a mockery that it should be guaged by the monkey intellects of the tubrattlers of the day. Half the world says Montalembest, has received the Faith from the stream that had its rise in Britain. If the powers of the human mind be requisitioned to tell the Truth, they will declare that the British Empire could not have been erected without the union of the English Church and State. The product of the alliance is written in legible lines upon the Englishman's character. He respects Christianity as no other nation has ever respected it, he keeps the Sabbath as only the Jews ever kept it, whilst the marriage laws under which he lives are the re-duplications of the Commandment. His sense of justice and love of chivalry and fair play are the embodiment of the principles into which he was born. His bravery is not allied to Fate, but is the demonstration of a propensity that has bequeathed to Life its tributes of respect and offerings of admiration. Other nations fight for glory and are demoralized by defeat, but the Britishers' determination develops in strength as he discovers that little is to be gained by his death. The last to engage in war and the last to proclaim peace, the Englishman only fights for principles that are immortal. He appeals to Reason as the only human arbitrament of Truth, and rejects every claim that aspires to rise above its merits. His characteristics are precisely what the union of Church and State might be expected to make them. Environment has not only created his character, but has compelled it to prevent the English Church or State from falling below its own Ideal. On the one hand, his principles compelled him to inaugurate the Revolutions of 1645 and 1688, and on the other, to establish a religious Revolution under the Leaderships of Wesley and Whitfield. Not only is our Parliamentary Government the crystallizations of the union of Church and State, not only has it been purified and developed by the degree of perception with which Englishmen have read the Articles of the National Church, but other nations have been led to copy its forms into the regulations under which they themselves are governed. But if the establishment of the English national Faith has been materialized and embodied into the actions of Englishmen, if it has demonstrated to mankind that the Commandments are binding upon all Time, and that they cannot be corporeally observed without the union of Church and State, it is worthy of the respect and reverence that downtrodden nations have conceived for our country's character. If the Laws of Europe are based upon the Reformed Jurisprudence of Tribonian and his allies it is equally certain that the Laws of England are destined to become the foundations of the future Laws of the World. We see the prospective result in the nearer approximation of national Liberty to the English Ideal. We see it in the dread and jealousy of British influence as at present exemplified in the world, and of the desire of autocracies to

break it down, The English State has been raised to
higher conceptions of its duty and value as the result of
its union with the Church, whilst the Church has been
exalted to the highest pinnacle of responsibility and power
as the consequence of its connection with the State. The
majority of great Englishmen have been proud to belong to
our national communion, whilst the charms of her comprehensive genius have succeeded in winning the major
portion of English Legislative and executive genius to her
side. Genius itself may be erratic, but its highest forms will
be found to have a natural love for association with expressed embodiments of power. The authoritative definition of the visible Church of Christ that is incorporated in
Thirty-nine Articles of Religion has been accepted by the
major portion of the Churches of the world. Is the history
of Nonconformity anything more than a succession of pro-
tests against the attempts that have have made to obliterate
and to change that Article as the characteristic expression
of England's Faith? Is it not true that out of the two
hundred and fifty Nonconformist Denominations in the
country, only a single one owes its origin to the belief that
National Churches are unscriptural and therefore unlawful?
Has Dissent contributed as much to the Temple of Thought
as the Church of England has done? Have the shelves of
Christian Libraries been filled equally by Dissenters as by
National Churchmen during the past two hundred years?
Even if Dissent were based upon the new conception of its
principles, it would still be true that it can only claim to
have produced a minority of great British theologians and
thinkers. Nonconformity has done its full share of practical Christian work, and is valuable as a protest against the
various attempts that have been made to change the organized expression of our National creed, but its recent attempted degradation of the powers of the State has alienated
the bulk of modern English intellect from sympathy with
its communion. And yet it must not be forgotten that

British Nonconformity has benefitted immensely from the continuance of the union of Church and State. Without that alliance, Dissent would long since have become but the incongruous assimilation of ideas that are the bequests of units and obscure social sections. Such a result would be demanded of the fact that Christianity inculcates a change of life from its professors, and that its demands will continue to be only comparatively obeyed by the majority of men until the millenium. What would become of the social and political power of Nonconformity if arrested by the opposition of larger bodies of men acting under a different form of environment? What would then be its advocacy of a more rigid enforcement of the obligations of the Fourth Commandment, of its impugnation of the legalisation of vice in the British Empire, of its desire to penalize the use of oaths in public thoroughfares, of its defence and application of the laws of Bigamy and Divorce, of its craving for making the Nonconformist conscience a factor of the National Life of England? One turns away with disgust at the flightiness of irresponsible men who draw conclusions from a cursory examination of great questions which they have not probed and to which they have contributed no thought. The earlier Dissenters applied their reason to the elucidation of these weighty matters, and did not scruple to defend the principle of the union of Church and State. The new environment of Liberationism has blinded the eyes of living men to the fact that Cromwell and Pym were both believers in the necessity for maintaining the National Church of their country. ' Cromwell saw the need of administrative Reform in Church and State,' says Green in his History of the English people, 'but he had no sympathy whatever with the revolutionary theories which were filling the air around him. *He was still for an established Church, for a parochial system, and a ministry maintained by tithes.*' Howe, Flavel, Bagster, Doddridge, Gill, Matthew Henry, and the other Nonconformist Divines of the reigns of Charles the Second and his brother James were all likewise believers in the principle of the connection between Church and State. Wesley and Rowland Hill defended the maxim in later times. ' But has it not always been the opinion of the most spiritually minded persons that National religious establishments are unlawful ? *To far from it, answers Dr. Chalmers, the objection is only of modern growth. The first Dissenters never thought so.*' Why, therefore, have living Nonconformists turned their backs upon the principles of the founders of Nonconformity ? The answer is allied to the causes that have produced the history of the world. The environment of Liberationism has succeeded in crystallizing its forces around the Nonconformist conscience and has destroyed its apprehension of pure Reason. The stream of tendency is carrying the modern Dissenter to an ocean that he knows not of, and that he would see and avoid if he could only release himself from the grip of Fate. Civilized States must either rise to an appreciation of the objects for which they were created or sink to become the detractors of the struggle between good and evil that is perennially evolving in the lives of men. They must either lend the weight of their subjugating Imageries to the development of opinion into corporate act of religious Life, or scatter their sporules over minds that will reproduce, expand, and diffuse their degraded apprehensions. The freedom of the human will has predestined one of these two results, and will continue to do so until it shall cease to belong to a type of Life that has fallen from its Ideal. History lifts the veil from the Imageries that have subdued the rectitude of the world to shew us the sleeping places of the nations and Empires of the dead. It is a solemn scene and resplendant with glimpses of the chasm that divides Time from Eternity. A flood of purple light shoots across the globe of Death to decipher the tributes of warning that fire their majestic meanings into the souls of living men. The porticos of memory invite us to partake of their shelter as they dazzle our minds with their bewildering enchantments of sapphire and gold. And we sink to a sleep from which we shall only be awakened by the dreams of a lost heritage and the echoes of our own despair. If England should be numbered with the nations that have received the Truth and lost it again, then indeed will her star have set in the ruin of the mightiest Empire that the world has ever seen.

Chapter VI.

OPINION VERSUS RULE OF LIFE.

'The most important fact to every man,' says Froude in his life of Beaconsfield, 'is his religion. If we would know what man is we ask what notions he has formed about his duty to man and God.' The historian's apophthegm is true both of men and of nations. Religion is the parent of conduct everywhere. A Turk, a Hindoo, a Chinese, an Englishman is precisely what his religion has made him. But as Christianity is a spiritual religion and is allied both to the Church militant and the Church triumphant there must be a line of demarcation between its real and its nominal attachees. Can that line be drawn by any living man? We trow not. The majority of the three hundred and fifty millions of the people of Europe would be deeply offended if told that they were not Christians. They conform to their creeds everywhere, and they rise and fall in the religious scale in accordance with the demands that are made upon them. As we belong to no higher type of life than themselves we have no right to say whether or not they are worthy of the name that they bear. Environment has everywhere made them what they are and will make them what they are to become so long as the human will shall continue to be free. Christendom is ubiquitous but its surface does not present a common form and character. England and Sweden differ from Spain and Italy as much as Ireland differs from Wales. These contradistinctions and differences of feature are positive proofs that they have been produced by the idiosyncrasies of environment and differentiating strengths of human wills.

Character in religion as in everything else is the materialized semblance of its surroundings. A word is sufficient to dispel the belief that the Kingdom of Grace operates to compel mankind to turn to God. The Kingdom of Grace cannot operate outside the borderland of Revelation without destroying the character of Revelation itself, and as three fourths of the world are not yet even nominal adherents of Christianity so they cannot be influenced by the Kingdom of Grace even to the slightest degree. Catholic environment produces Catholic character as Protestant environment produces at least an outward conformity to Protestant character. The dicta of Catholicity are obeyed because they are the Imageries of power even when they refuse to submit themselves to an examination by the faculty of Reason. Catholic opinion is the Rule of Catholic life everywhere. And what is true of Catholicism is also true of Greek Christianity. The Russian is outwardly the most religious man in the world. His devotion is persistent and goes as far as his environment induces it to go. He is reminded by the glitter of his Church domes, by the ecclesiastical paintings that adorn the street corners and open spaces of his towns, by the respect that has for centuries been paid to his Priests, by the gesticulations of his ornate subjugating Church services, and by the silver glitter of the sacred Volume whose covers he is commanded to kiss, that his Church demands the measure of obedience that is represented by these symbols from his life. He is content to deserve merit from his acquiescence and to let his intellectualities lie dormant at the request of materialized subversive powers. He is pliant as a babe because his will power is still that of a child. The ninety five per cent of Muscovites who can neither read nor write are blocks of flesh and bone upon whose visages have been carved the Imageries of environment. What is true of Greek and Western Christianity is likewise true of Protestant states. Sweden is polished beyond compare because its National

Liturgy has made no compromise with error in its appeals to the highest development of the powers of human Reason. The canaille of the United States of America are boisterous in their protestations of Liberty and License because their secular surroundings have not been tamed by the union of Church and State. The fourth of July celebrations both proclaim the birth of American Independence and the advent of an environment that was to secularize the major portion of the character of America. The War of Independence resolved American society into its component parts and gave it new conceptions of Life and of the object for which it was bequeathed to the world. New hopes destroyed the traditions of the past and bequeathed new avenues of secularized thought to the American people. The goal of the new ambition was not perceived because of the temporary aberration of Religious Thought and of the desire to obliterate the memories of the country's past. The State was shorn of its highest functions and reduced to temporal dominion and power. Liberty and License were raised aloft as the only objects of adoration—the Ideals that should subvert the nobler Imageries of social units and religious sections. American statesmen made ample provision for the fructification of the pleasures of Life but forgot that all materialized forms of social power were created to direct human thought towards the majestic certainties of the Life to come. The American nation was drilled to intertwine one formula into the fibres and tissues of its being and never to forget that England whipped the world and America whipped England. The child absorbs ideas but to develop and to reproduce them again in after life. What Admiral Sampson learned in his youthful days he developed in a despatch that was to become the possession of history: '*I present to the nation as a fourth of July offering* the destruction of Admiral Cerveras fleet.' Nelson would probably have offered the victory of the Nile to the English nation as a birthday present if his character had been formed under a similar national environment. The grandeur of American life and Institutions will never be complete until she moderates the preponderating influences of the State by uniting it to one or more branches of the Church. A slavish servility is no more degrading to true manhood than untamed wills running amuck with the authority of License. The former is the characteristic of the canaille of Spain, Austria, and Russia, the latter the designation of the rabble of America. What can our conceptions of Truth be but the standards of moral principles by which we are surrounded? What is the yellow journalism of the United States but the creation of an environment that for a hundred years has recognized no moral obligation? 'Redshid,' says Disraeli in one of his letters to his sister, 'was an approved warrior, a consummate politician, *unrivalled as a dissembler in a country where dissimulation is part of the moral culture?'* When the Emperor Nicholas wished to convey his impression of the highest degree of personal loyalty and honour *he always spoke of the word of an English gentleman.* Environment either blunts our inhibition of the Truth or impresses its sacredness upon our minds. The new life that was born of American independence was destined to make it impossible for the commandments to be corporeally incorporated in the life of the nation. The thunders of Sinai were but to be re-echoed by the inaudible whisperings of American conscience. The American Sunday therefore fell, and the American laws of marriage, bigamy, and Divorce sank to become the amenabilities of private accommodation. A century has passed away and American politics have become a byword and a reproach to the thinking portion of the American people. Marriage Licences are taken out to make flirtations respectable and when the ceremony has been performed sometimes in plumbers' stores and sometimes in Lions' dens, the first passing Judge is called upon to untie the Knot and to say adieu to the fun of the Romance. When life is thus played with we cannot wonder that the American revolver arrests its progress or that the murderer is acquitted and but cautioned not again to run foul of his country's licence. The bulk of human acts are but the materializations of our environments, the reduplication of principles that lie at the root of our social ceremonies. American life is what it was made by the men who framed the constitution of America just over a hundred years ago. It may, however, be retorted that the British colonies do not possess National Churches and that their characters should therefore approximate to those of the citizens of America. We reply that the colonies are allied to a Power whose character has been formed by the union of Church and State, and that the colonies have reflected and will continue to reflect the disposition of the present State. Were the colonies to sever themselves from Britain tomorrow their characters would immediately change. The British colonies are parts of an Empire of which England is the corner stone. The whole is greater than its part. They are affected by the public opinion and Rule of Life that obtain in Britain. London is more the capital of New South Wales than Sydney, of Victoria than Melbourne, of South Australia than Adelaide, and of Van Diemens Land than Hobart Town. The Public Opinion of England is the Public Opinion of Nova Scotia, New Brunswick, Manitoba, British Columbia, Vancouver, and Prince Edward's Islands Pietermanitzberg and Cape Town. Can it be denied that the public opinion of England was also the opinion of America before the War of Independence? When England changes her environment the other parts of the Empire will change theirs too. When England ceases to merge opinion into Rule of Life the colonies will cease to do so too. The differences between Britain and her colonies with regard to environment are not of principle but of Degree. As the parts of England herself are affected in various ways by the inequalities of ecclesiastical endowment so are the provinces of the colonies

affected similarly too. As the old parts of England are
better endowed than the new are the older parts of the
colonies are frequently provided with religious establishments when the newer places have no Churches at all. This
fact was pointed out in the House of Commons by Sir
Michael H. Beach in a discussion upon the Welsh Suspensory
Bill some four or five years ago. The Backwoodsman of
Australia is the creation of his environment and is known
to frequently fall to the level of Paganism for want of
Images or Institutions to keep his conscience alive. It
matters not what nation he may belong to, he becomes the
embodiment of the principles by which he is surrounded.
The wills of individuals and nations are poised on the same
Throne of Light and are either strengthened or weakened
by the operation of the same persistent laws. The per-
manent characteristics of men are only those than can be
brought out by opposition, and that appertain more to
brutes than to the domains of moral virtue. Englishmen
can be effectually corrupted though less easily than other
nations because of the hereditary propensities of their
country's environment. The belief that Englishmen can
never fall away from a nominal profession of Christianity,
that its practical principles have been incorporated into
their natures, and that no laws can be sufficiently powerful
to turn their country to the profession of another Faith, is
one of the delusions of the age in which we live. It is
indeed a doubly distilled delusion because it is held by
schools of thought that are as divergent as the Poles. One
class of thinkers declare that Legislation cannot injure or
destroy the Religion of Britain because it is miraculously
maintained by the Kingdoms of Providence and Grace,
whilst another type of exegetical opinion avows that our
Christianity cannot be hurt because it is in the safe keeping
of men who are in the line of the apostolic succession. If it
be true that like causes produce like effects it must be true
that both conceptions are opposed to the laws of nature, the

[E]

causes of the will's freedom, and the teaching of human history. Again and again have Englishmen surrendered every national characteristic to become brutes and autocrats of injustice and cruelty. Hume's story of the Irish Rebellion of 1641 may be quoted in substantiation of this great historic fact. 'The English,' says he, 'as heretics abhorred of God, were marked out for slaughter. The English colonies were almost annihilated in the open country of Ulster whence the flames of rebellion diffused themselves over the three other provinces of Ireland. Not content with repelling the English from their houses, and despoiling them of their manors and cultivated fields, the Irish stripped them of their clothes, and turned them out, naked and defenceless, to all the inclemency of the Season. The number of those who perished is estimated at the lowest at from 30,000 to 40,000. The English of the Pale or ancient English planters, who were all catholics, were probably not at first in the secret and pretended to blame the insurrection and detest the barbarity with which it was accompanied. By their protestations and declarations they engaged the Justices to supply them with arms which they promised to employ in defence of the government, but in a little time the interests of Religion were found more powerful than regard and duty to their mother country. They chose Lord Gormanston their leader, *and joining the old Irish, rivalled them in every act of violence towards the English Protestants.*' Another proof of the fact of which the foregoing quotation is an evidence is afforded by the story of the Indian mutiny. 'If ever the crisis found the man,' says M'Carthy, 'Lord Canning was the man called for by that crisis in India. Because he would not listen to the bloodthirsty clamours of mere frenzy, he was nicknamed "Clemency Canning." Indeed for some time people wrote and spoke, not merely in India but in England, as if clemency were a thing to be reprobated, like treason or crime. For a while it seemed a question of patriotism which would propose the most savage

and sanguinary measures of revenge. If such a temper
were encouraged said Disraeli we ought to take down from
our altars the image of Christ and raise the statue of Moloch
there. If people were so carried away in England, whence
the danger was far remote, we can easily imagine what were
the fears and passions roused in India itself. The taking
of Delhi was followed by an act of unpardonable bloodshed.
Hudson went boldly to the tomb whence the King and his
family had taken refuge, tried them as rebels taken red-
handed, and borrowing a carbine from one of his troopers, he
shot them dead with his own hand. Nicholson was one of
the honest and most capable officers whom the war produced.
It is worthy of record as an evidence of the temper aroused
even in men from whom better things might have been
expected, that Nicholson strongly urged the passing of a
law to authorize flaying alive, impalement, or burning of
the murderers of the women and children in Delhi. He
urged this view again and again, and deliberately argued it
on grounds alike of policy and principle.' History and
experience are both replete with evidence of the fact that
Englishmen's characters have been changed by the operations of environment. And lest it should be thought that
the examples quoted do not and cannot apply to our own
age we will prove our point by citing some of the biograph-
ical episodes of living men. One of the most brilliant of
contemporary journalists recently went abroad to study the
Land of the Crysanthemum and to marry a lady of Japan.
She was an adherent of the Shinto faith which is a mere
bagatelle in the world's economics, but she speedily secured
the conversion of her husband to Shintoism. A living
son and heir to an English Earldom is now known to
have adopted the religion of Buddha. An existing British
Nobleman married a Spanish lady at Seville and is now a
believer in the doctrines of Mohammed. A grand daughter
of the most brilliant English poet of the nineteenth century
is also now a follower of the prophet of Mecca. The late

Lady Hesther Stanhope and the Countess of Ellenborough both died in the faith of Islam. The widowed Countess of Stamford has since the death of her husband followed the Pagan belief of her tribe, and worshipped all kinds of horrible heathen deities, while the present Lord Gardner, his wife, and children are all Brahmins. The foregoing particulars were published in Mr. O'Connor's society paper for the month of October, 1898, and they demonstrate to the hilt that Englishmen like the members of other nations are but the creations of their environment. There was as much truth as sarcasm in Lord Beaconsfield's remarks when informed that the Zulus had killed the Prince Imperial in South Africa. 'A very remarkable people the Zulus:' said he, ' they defeat our generals, *they convert our Bishops*, they have settled the fate of a great European dynasty.' But we need not go to history or to biography for proofs of the fact that the beliefs and actions of our countrymen are affected by their environments. Every traveller has noticed the coincidences and appurtenances of this fact in his own life and in the lives of his countrymen whom he has met abroad. If British mercantile sailors convey a false estimate of English character to the nations of the world it is solely because they are the embodiments of their indifferent surroundings. Twenty thousand of them are believed to live on ships that are never darkened by religious services. Five hundred Englishmen and Scotchmen approximately were engaged by the Spanish Government to build Admiral Cervera's ill-tarred fleet at Bilbao about seven years ago, but during their residence in Spain they could not be prevailed upon by the English chaplain of the Port to attend the services of the local Church or to remember the Christian ethics that they had left at home. We also speak from experience when we refer to the case of the few Britishers who still reside at Archangel in Northern Russia. Their religious conduct and belief are apparently the reduplication of their surroundings and the English summer chaplain of

the Port has to chronicle the fact that he cannot induce
them to attend his religious services. 'Irishmen,' says
Froude, ' obey authority and prosper under it: *But they
run wild when left to their own wills.*' What the historian
says of Irishmen in their natural capacities is true of all
men in their religious inclinations. Free wills will only
respond to the Images of Authority by which they are
surrounded. The State was created to make these Images
the highest object of its care and to give them the noblest
position for materializing their influences in the creeds and
lives of men. Neither human nor Divine Laws will be
heeded by the majority of men unless they are symbolized
by the majesty of created visible power. England has
advanced our globe's courses by her correct perceptions of
Revelation, experience, and history : she has demonstrated
that the commandments cannot be corporeally obeyed
without the Union of Church and State : she will undo her
work and retard the progress of Christianity by reducing
the State to a degraded position in the natural economies.
The Liberationist will not learn the abhorrencies of his
principles so long as he remains under the environment of
Liberationism but he will succeed in running foul to the
teachings of human history. The men who play before the
footlights of England's destiny have problems to solve that
are red with ruin and bright as the Light of eternity, and it
is for them to decide whether the world's career shall be
changed or the British Empire be commissioned to accelerate
the advent of the Kingdom of God.

CHAPTER VII

WHAT WILL BE THE EFFECTS OF DISESTABLISHMENT UPON ENGLAND AND THE WORLD?

Half a century ago the people of the British Empire were startled to hear that a society had just been formed in London for the purpose of securing the secularization of the State by the Disestablishment of the Churches of England, Scotland, and Wales. We cannot fully comprehend the indignant feelings with which the announcement was received because the danger has long since crystallized itself into the environment of our lives. Men are now trained to propagate the belief that Disestablishment is essentially a desirable Reform. Reason, however, tells us that the germs of peril must be inherent in any proposal that threatens to destroy the fundamental maxims of a nation's character and greatness. The maintenance of the Established Church was as sacred to the Nonconformists and Churchmen who lived before the advent of the Liberation Society as the defence of the Monarchy is to the men of to-day and as the Act of Union was to the voters of all schools of thought who exercised the Franchise before the Radical Party sold itself to the enemies of its country. The success that has attended the assailment of the cardinal principles of a nation's character in the past has, however, taught us that vital principles may be safely attacked whenever the organizers of the Revolution are prepared to explain away the first presentiments of fear and surprise. As familiarity with physical danger causes us to forget its perils so does intimacy with Revolutionary political principles induce us to obliviate their mighty issues upon the fortunes of the world. But the danger will remain long after the memories of it have passed away. A Revolution has assumed the garb of Reform and under its new habiliment has captured the Reasons of living men. As we have ceased to disregard the perils to Christianity that are involved in the secularization of the English state so will our children complete the issue by assaulting principles that we ourselves still know to be essential to the preservation of our national life. We laugh at Socialism and Anarchy to-day but who will dare affirm that their tenets will not be adopted by the next generation of Englishmen? A shortsighted policy Disestablished the Irish Church thirty years ago and thought that the event would make Ireland happy. Vain delusion! Nemesis has followed in the wake of the blunder and has made Irishmen more determined than ever to secede from a Protestant Union and to ally themselves to some Roman Catholic State. By the determination not to perceive the natural consequences of individual and national acts do nations fall and empires decline and die. We live in a conventional age and allow our perceptions to be dazzled, blinded, and destroyed by the maxims of Revolution that come to us in the garb of Reforms. We occupy the trysting places between the propagation of false beliefs and the ubiquity of ruin into which they are about to plunge. The provinces of history are to warn us of danger but not to interfere with the free workings of the human will. We have the same power to inaugurate Revolutions, to destroy empires, and to divert the causes of human history as was possessed by the nations of a mighty past. As they had prescience which they did not utilize so have we futurities that we can change, vary, alternate, or destroy. Let us not forget that the freedom of the human will is to last until the millenium. As Liberationism has destroyed our Reasons in the past so have we little or no hope that it will fail to do so in the future. We may therefore rest assured that Disestablishment will not cease to be advocated by the persistent proclamation that it is a Desideratum and a Potential Reform. What then will be the effects of Disestablishment upon Great Britain and the world ? Can they be enumerated by any man who is alive to-day ? Freeman has summarized the direct effects that will accrue from the severance of the Union between the English Church and State, but neither an individual nor a generation of men can total the indirect issues of the adoption of such a retrograde policy. 'We should,' says Freeman, ' have to repeal all laws by which the Established Church is recognized in a way in which other Religious bodies are not recognized. The Ruler of the whole nation must no longer even seem to be admitted to the royal office by the ministers of a religious body which forms only part of the nation. The obligation on the part of the Sovereign to be in communion with what is now the Established Church must be taken away. A Popish King must become lawful as well as an Independent or Baptist King. The King may doubtless have his chapel and his chaplains of any persuasion that he pleases, but they must no longer keep about them anything of the character of a public Institution. The Bishops must of course lose their seats in the House of Lords. Ecclesiastical courts must come to an end and with them must come to an end the appeal from the ecclesiastical courts to the privy council. The convocations of the two Provinces must be left as free as the Wesleyan Conference. The Crown must no longer have the appointment to the many ecclesiastical offices which are now in its gift. . . . All laws must be repealed which treat the Church or its fabrics as national Institutions. Their could be no more questions about burial bills, about Dissenting Churchwardens and the like. Disestablishment must cut both ways. If it abolishes privilage it must abolish bondage. There must be no payments out of public funds, out of taxes or rates, for any religious purpose. There must be no such thing as a chaplain of a ship, or of a regiment, of a gaol, an asylum, or a

workhouse, or of the House of Commons itself.' Such is
the long list of prospective ecclesiastical changes that the
historian has enumerated for the especial edification of the
Liberationists of Great Britain. But will any man with an
insight into human nature avow that it is possible for these
changes to be adopted without bringing in a longer list of
unperceived accretions and desuetudes in their train ? A
device that aspires to destroy the allegiance which a nation
has placed at the disposal of the Almighty for so many
hundreds of years and to replace it by no design save the
accidental incoherencies of units and obscure social sections
must develop into an iconoclasm that will break down the
Images of Christian tendency that have bequeathed the
causes of a mighty Empire's Faith to the world. Great
principles cannot be tampered with without destroying the
confidence that they have begotten, the stately representa-
tions that have environed and produced a nations character.
Disestablishment cannot be freed from the natural tendencies
of movement, or prevented from eclipsing its perceived
material issues. The sins of the fathers are only visited
upon the children because the fathers' lives are too short to
restrict the penalty to themselves. The conscientious Dis-
establisher judges human events by the standard of his own
life and fails to comprehend the expansion of principles that
are co-extensive with the life of the world. The results of
the secularization of the State will not be seen by a single
generation because they cannot be robbed of their propensity
to expand. Disestablishment will be a Revolution in itself
because England can produce no precedent for such an act.
The Englishmen of the future will be born under a secular
Colossus and will become by nature the duplications of its
materializing inclinations. Men who will live under the all
powerful laws of a civil environment will naturally ask
whether Christianity is more of a Revelation than the other
religious systems of the world. Scepticism will advance in
England as it has never been permitted to advance before.

Even the Faith of the Churches will shrink from the perception of eternal consequences when they transcend the lowest standard of degraded life in this world. The Preacher's message will be shorn of its semblances of authority and will be less judged by its fidelity and Truth than by its intellectual skill. The falsehood that is proclaimed by Rhetoricians and Rhapsodists will be believed before the Truth that is spoken by ordinary men. Liberationism will snap asunder the chains that for two centuries have galled the intellects of Unitarians in England and have made them the iconoclasts of national representative power. The Incumbent and the Free Minister will become the products of an equality that will reduce them both to a lower common level. The social prestige that has driven home the message of the Established Minister when the Dissenter has failed to get an audience of the Conscience will have been taken over by the materialized semblances of secularism and Infidelity. Nonconformity itself will be spurned as the representation of a bigoted little social class. Disestablishment will hand over the keys of power to the seething masses who will profess no Religion and whose first object will be to complete the secularization of the State. For as the British Reformers were the first to perceive that the Commandments were meant for all time and that they could only be corporeally obeyed by the Union of Church and State, so will the Liberation Society succeed in demoralizing the observance of the moral law and in relegating it to the domains of the individual conscience. Thus will it be legal to do anything on the Sabbath which it is not illegal to do on the other days of the week. Thus will men be allowed to have the same privileges of Divorce in England as are at present enjoyed by the Libertines of America. If the State was created for secular purposes only as the Liberationist avows who, may we ask, is justified in asking it to bolster up a Religious law? If the Image of power was never constructed to assist in the promulgation

of the Christian Faith what right have we to attempt to
change its instituted character? Will worldly men allow
the smaller number of professing Christians to attach a
religious Incubus to a State which has just been freed from
its bondage and raised to its Ideal? The certainty of a
negative reply will be brought home to the citizens of the
Empire more forcibly than they have ever thought to be
possible. A Secular State can no more rise above its secular-
ity than a stream can rise above its source. Disestablishment must be followed by the repeal of all laws that have a
religious base and that compel the nation to carry out the
Commandments in its corporate character. Thus will the
success of Liberationism be followed by the downfall of the
English Sunday and by the repeal of the present laws of
marriage, Divorce, and Bigamy. The laws of nature are
uniform in their character and what they do not condemn
in America and Turkey they will not condemn in England.
Our Sunday Societies, Halls of Science, and Freethinking
Assemblies will redouble their efforts to secure Disestablishment as the potentiality of the event unfolds itself to their
view. Their inconsistency would be as apparent by the
adoption of any opposite course of action as is the inconsistency of professing Christians in advocating the secularization of the State today. The Liberation Society has laboured
for fifty years to degrade the English State, but it may wish
to labour for ever to restore it to its Divinely appointed
position again. But if Disestablishment be fraught with
danger to England it is still more replete with peril to the
other countries of the world. Every age must be kept up
to a sense of its moral responsibilities by an Ideal to whose
heights it cannot attain. Great Britain has been the world's
Ideal for three centuries and a half and will remain so until
Disestablishment shall have changed its national character
and overthrown its noblest Institutions. A moral shock to
the faith of England must of necessity be felt by the other
countries of the globe. The future will then draw a new

Inspiration from the Hand that rules the world. The lodestar of history can only cease to shine when it has been eclipsed by a more resplendent effulgency. A Statesman, a Martyr, a Kingdom or an Empire will be requisitioned to hold aloft the memorials of the world's destiny when England may have been numbered with the forces of the dead. The destinies will fight for the attainment of the eternal purposes whether they be corporealized into representative Aureoles or burning Diadems. The consciousness of thought cannot be destroyed by apostate Kingdoms because it is refurnished by the Providence of God. Egypt, Assyria, Persia, Greece, Macedonia, Arabia, Spain, England, wear the mantle of Empire in turn and pass it on as if it were but the semblances of a dream. England is both the last and the greatest of the Immortals and the tramp of her destiny is the echo of the trumpet blast that sounds the ruin of a fallen world.

CHAPTER VIII.

THE KINGDOMS OF PROVIDENCE AND GRACE.

There is a tinge of loveliness about spiritual Christianity that meets the highest aspirations of the soul. Men who live more in eternity than in Time wear a habiliment of character that is unequalled in the world. Every act that they perform is a memorial of the Judgment Day. Every thought that they conceive is developed or suppressed according to its affinity to the will of God. Such men are to be found in every age and country and will continue to rise above the ruins of human nature until Time shall be no more. They are the personifications of Lives that have really been born again. The policies of Kingdoms and States have only an academic and hypothetical interest for them excepting as they tend to speed the coming of the Kingdom of God. Faith is the compass of such men's lives, the decree at whose bidding they are prepared to live or to die. Spirituality has taken such a hold upon them that they cannot discuss mundane matters like other men. Their presence in the churches is both a lever for the development of spiritual life and for degrading Reason and mentality as aids to the perception of the decrees of Truth in the world. The Knowledge that the Wesleyan Church is blessed with more than its proportion of such men caused the Ruling President of the Wesleyan Conference in his inaugural address to plead for the outpouring of a little more sanctified common sense amongst the members of his communion. It is in no spirit of captious criticism that we re-echo the President's prayer and apply its covenants to a deeper consideration of the question relating to Disestablishment in

England, Scotland, and Wales. For the spirtually minded members of the Liberation Society who have abjured the functions of human Reason are known to avow that no human act can injure the Christian Church because it is under the especial care of God. They ward off all warnings with a phrase and escape the dangers of every conclusion with a period and a term. They tell us that Disestablishment is desirable because it will remove the trammels that appear to have shorn a spiritual Church of its spiritual character. They forget that the Church upon earth is composed of living men, and that living men are the interpreters of the laws of nature. They fail to remember that spirituality in its essence is beyond the reach of fallen human nature and that its degrees of attainment are not restricted by the materialization of purpose and effect. Their attitude precludes all appeals to Reason as aids to Truth and makes the history of Christianity a miraculous interference with the operations of the natural law. Their assertion has undoubtedly given an Impetus to Disestablishment that would have appalled the Fathers of Nonconformity. But with the hope that the prayer of the Wesleyan President has been answered and that his friends have been blessed with a large measure of sanctified common sense ere now, we will proceed to demonstrate that the assertion runs foul to the objects of Revelation and to the records of human history. The laws of nature are uniform in their operations throughout the world and they do not bend the human will in one part of the globe unless they bend it wherever it may be found. If the functions of the Kingdom of Grace are legislative in Christendom they are likewise legislative in all parts of the world. If their object is to turn men to God by force or to interfere with the operations of the natural law they must seek the same results in Christian and heathen countries alike. Hence the absurdity of supposing that the Christian Church cannot be influenced by the actions of the natural law. The very fact that only a small proportion of the inhabitants of Christendom endeavour to make their lives the reflex of Divine decrees, or even rise above the propensity of acknowledging the existence of the Kingdom of Grace, clearly demonstrates that the militant Church is influenced by the same accidents and to the same degree as the remaining social forces of the world. The laws of nature are the expression of the Almighty power and are uninfluenced by the rise and fall of the religious beliefs of men. They operate as regularly and powerfully amongst barbarisms as amongst civilizations and pay the same court to heathen as to Christian countries. We know nevertheless that Christianity is a Revelation and must therefore have some affinity to the object for which the world was created. Wherein therefore is it under the especial care of the Creator and under what conditions can His miraculous intervention be conceived? The powers of the human mind were given us to unravel this problem of human life. The Records of the world declare that the guardianship which God exercises over the Church is constant in its care but intermittent in its operation, and is determined by the extent of the danger that threatens the Church's welfare. We may be certain that it will be exercised to prevent the annihilation of the Revealed will in the world, and to thwart any human effort that may be put forth to obscure the majesty of its glory. In respect to these two events the promise has been verified in the annals of human history. 'Lo I am with you even to the end of the world.' If the degradation of the English State by the Disestablishment of the Church does not imply the progeneration of either of these evils we may rest assured that its consequences will not be arrested or destroyed by the Hand of God. Miracles can be compreprehended by Faith but not by Reason but they will be rendered all the more difficult to believe by the attempt that has been made to import them into the issues of the Disestablishment question. No extraordinary prescience is

required to perceive that there is an analogy between the
faults of Liberationist belief in regard to miracles and
the blunder that was made by Hume in relationship to the
same question. We may here pause to ask whether the
Dissenting degeneracy of Hume's Century would have sur-
vived its own alternation had it not been encrusted with the
environment of a Church that could not hereticate because
of its alliance with the State. 'The laws of nature were
uniform,' said Hume, and in any given instance it was more
likely as a mere matter of evidence that men should deceive
or be deceived than that those laws should have been
deviated from. Newman was so satisfied with Hume's
proposition that he told a body of Undergraduates at
Oxford that it could not be assailed. But as a matter of
fact it is no more difficult of assault than is the Liberationist
position today. For what object were the laws of nature
made uniform? If for no object at all how can the belief
in their uniformity be established? Did Hume perceive an
effect without gauging a cause, if so, is he not condemned
by the postulates and axioms of pure Reason and of Spinoza?
To understand an effect,' says the great Pantheist in his
ethica, ' *implies that we understand the cause of it. And if
there be no given cause no effect can follow.*' If the Disciples
perceived both cause and effect with regard to the uniformity
of nature's laws *it was less likely* that they should have been
deceived than that those laws should have been deviated
from. As those laws were created to be the expression of
the Creator's power so was their suspension demanded for
the establishment of the belief in that Power and in its
development in the institution of Christianity. It was
necessary that the uniformity of nature's laws should be
deviated from for the purpose of attesting the character of
Revelation, of diverting the streams of human tendency
when tottering before the upheaval of the Mohammedan
conquests, and of resuscitating the spiritual character of the
Church when obscured by the encroachments, assumptions,

and blasphemies of men at the time of the Reformation. Thus has the promise been splendidly fulfilled, 'Lo I am with you even to the end of the world.' The Gospel miracles served a purpose that differed only in degree from the results of the battle of Tours and from the establishment of the Protestant Reformation. We therefore see that Hume conceived wrong impressions of the miracles and their import on the one hand and that the spiritually minded Liberationist has apprehended false ideas concerning them on the other. Faith and Reason must be allied for the comprehension of Disestablishment and its issues in the future of the Empire and of the world. Human history bears witness to the fact that Christianity has been ejected from Kingdoms and States that were once so many bright jewels in its crown. What has become of the Provinces that bore witness to the lifework of such men as Cyprian, Tertullian, Augustine, Basil, and Chrysostom? What has become of the Christianity that was planted by Polycarp and Ignatius, by Papias, Quadratus, Aristides, Ariosto, Claudius Apollinaris, and Miltiades? Who now reveres the memories of Melito, Tatian of Assyria, Theophilus and Hermias? What do living men think of the venues of Nicea, Constantinople, Ephesus, and Chalcedon? Is it not strange that the countries in which were held the only general councils whose authority is acknowledged both by the Greek and Latin Churches should long since have ceased to be Christian? And is not the establishment of Mohammedanism upon the partial ruins of Christianity a complete answer to the men who declare that the Revealed Faith cannot be injured because it is under the especial care of God? Are not the records of its intermittent failures and successes so pronounced that some great minds have leaped to the opposite extreme and have declared its fortunes to be absolutely under the dominion of the human will? Was the sceptical historian of the last century more to be blamed for the injuries that he inflicted upon the Faith than men

[F]

who are now prepared to destroy the fortifications of the Church and to rely upon a miracle to subvert the natural consequences of their acts? We may rest assured that a miracle will not save England from the sequences of her folly unless Disestablishment predetermines the annihilation of Christianity in the world. England must either wear the mantle of greatness herself or transfer it to the guardianship of some more faithful country. It is axiomatically true that as States that were once Christian have ceased to be so, so may countries that are Christian today surrender their Faith tomorrow. There was more truth than cynicism in Bernard's address to the Knights Templars when handing them the Rules of the order : ' Under Divine Providence we do believe this new kind of religion was introduced by you in the holy places, that is to say, the Union of warfare with religion, so that religion, being armed, maketh her way by the sword, and smiteth the enemy without sin.' There is more faithfulness than expediency in declaring that Disestablishment will give a blow to Anglo Saxon Christianity such as it has never received before, and that the laws of nature will not be suspended to intercept its partial ruin. As Faith without works is dead so Faith without Reason is but the subversion of the highest faculties of the human mind. If these had not been created for a purpose they would not have been bequeathed to us at all. The germs of manhood must be fertilized by the currents of history or the evolution of humanity will be but the evolution of the world's ruin. Whatsoever a man soweth that shall he also reap even though the Kingdoms of Providence and Grace are powerful enough to determine a different type of award. The people of this generation shall not pass away until they have indited the beliefs of ages that are still to come.

CHAPTER IX.

THE POTENTIALITIES OF THE UNION BETWEEN THE ENGLISH CHURCH AND STATE.

The evolution of humanity is not an unbroken progress towards perfection. Philosophy degrades its perceptions when it declares that human history is the evolution of events which lie already in their causes as the properties of geometrical figures lie in the scientific definition of those figures. Nor is it true that the life of the individual man, the long sequel of his acts and fortunes, and all that he has done and is to do, till the type is exhausted and gives place to other combinations, is governed by laws as inherent and as necessary as those through which the mathematician develops his inferences from the equation of an ellipse. The lives of men and nations are what men and nations have made them by the substitution of opportunity for the faculties of pure Reason and the human will. The draft of the world might have been deleted of its protuberances of tyranny and shame. The Records of human history might have been more glorious than they are. Hegel, Schegel, and Comte have but touched the fringe of a conception that is capable of rehabilitating the annals of the world and furbishing them with the noblest Imageries of the soul. Man is both a moral agent and an animal and the life picture which he has bequeathed to his race is but the besmearment of mentality by the enterprises of his lower life. The highest monument of Time is but the abuse of the powers of volition ; the resolute forgetfulness of the great object for which Time itself was born. Had the

human capacity been bequeathed to another type of Life it
is possible that its evolution would have been an unbroken
progress towards perfection. Who can enumerate the advancements and retrocessions of human history, its remini-
scences and reviews, failures and successes, hopes and fears,
emulations and despairs, kindnesses and cruelties, civilizations and barbarism, reflexes of heaven, and rectoactives of
hell? Who can deny that human happiness has been taught
and bought for in the Infliction of human pain, and that
Dominion and Power have been utilized to extract Revenge
from the victimisation of the life that has dared to soar
above the materialization of the world's Ideal? Opportunism has been the guiding star of the ages and has shewn no
semblance of feeling save that of regret at the shadows of
Death that would continue to obtrude and to darken its
vicious ways. The centuries are dyed with the blood of
martyrs shed by types of Life that were no higher than
their own, and the tyrannies succumb only to progenerate
new forms of despotism and oppression. The hand of
cruelty is still raised to strike its kindred down. When will
the human race begin to learn that man was never destined
to circumvent the happiness of man? When will man
acknowledge that Empires as the highest form of created
power will be requistioned to wage terrific wars of justice in
the world so long as man continues to deny the equality of
man. Who can read the human story without wishing that
the human faculties had either been circumscribed or absolutely controlled by the Kingdoms of Providence and Grace.
Then would there have been no empires raised to enforce
the evolution of Eternity's Decrees, no vile governments to
be shattered for defending the cruel fanaticisics of human
faiths, no prejudicies to be stamped upon the wings of ages
to subdue, to wreck, and to destroy the use of the resplendent faculties of men. We reel beneath the memories of the
wrongs that still remain to be righted, the infernal conclusions that must not be questioned, the twelve hundred

millions of men who have brains but must not use them. We fall back before the sixty centuries of devilry that have turned the world's heritage to monstrosity and degradation. What a record for a mental endowment that was originally superior to that of the angels. Can it be true that evolution has not begun for three quarters of the peoples of the earth. Are there men breathing who are not allowed to think, question, to ask for authority, to answer their disbeliefs in material results that refuse to appeal either to their Faith or to their reason? Is their freedom ever to be secured and is it to be acquired by coherencies of brother men or by the thunderbolts of an insulted God? Are the heavens to be blackened with wrath as when the rebel angels were consigned to their doom or are the custodians of the present apportionment of Time to be inspired for the mighty fray? Are the men of the present generation to burn the encasements of the captured intellect of brother men in a fire of awful retribution? If so, is England destined to lead the van and to teach the world once and forever that there is no visible body on the face of this material globe to whose Decrees men must submit in the matter of private judgment? Never was her opportunity so great and glorious as it is to-day. Never was she offered such gigantic opportunities for bridging the chasms of the centuries and refurbishing the escutcheon of human thought that should have aided the Kingdoms of Providence and Grace to fire their Imperious decrees. Every age has to play its part in the evolution of humanity. Neither men nor nations can dissociate themselves from the Alpha and Omega of the human drama, from the genesis that works systematically to apportion the rewards of human right and wrong. We cannot forego our responsibilities, we must leave the world either better or worse than we found it. Great and little principles are alike troublesome to our love of repose, but they will continue to sting us into the consciousness that we are the units who have to produce the contemporary records of history. Ineptitude has made the via media as a compromise between truth and lies the only principle that the age thinks worth fighting for. The men or the society or the nation who still thinks that Truth should be made the life object of research is a butt for every fool's ridicule. No objection could be taken to this deplorable apathy if the world's destinies were to be evolved out of the idiosyncrasies of the human will alone. But every reflective mind knows that a bequeathed responsibility cannot rise above the demands that gave it birth and will not be allowed to lie dormant or to transmit degeneracy to the world without involving itself in its own ruin. Why are human Ideals so frequently broken down just as they appear to have been reached and to have been established? Why are Peace Societies so often forced to blush for their principles or to re-echo the martial strains of some just and necessary war? Has any Peace Society yet understood the trend of the world's events or perceived that wars will never be allowed by the Creator to cease until the human intellect shall be free to comprehend the importance of Revelation and of human destiny? As all men will have to account for the use which they have made of their talents so will nations and empires be raised and thrown down in Time according to their perception of their moral responsibilities. As it is with material wars so will it continue to be with the mental Revolutions that stamp the centuries with their Decrees. We shall be roused by their activities to a higher or a lower sense of accountability to the great object for which Time itself was born. The human race has broken its unity as a social order and the cleavage must be righted ere human fancies will be allowed to be raised to the position of national Ideals. The belief in human infallibilities, fanaticisms, and thaumaturgies must be destroyed ere the created powers shall be able to find the repose that they love so well. The fact that Truth is not supported by miraculous environment will never be allowed to excuse men from the responsibility of endeavouring to discover its Decretals. We smile as we sit around the craters of a volcano and seek safety in rest as its belching fires begin to redden the sky. England now stands before the footlights of the centuries to play her part in the evolution of humanity. What shall be the stamp of her contribution, the impress of her accord? Our countrymen can proclaim their creeds, avow their convictions, and promulgate their accession of advantage today as they never could before. And the freedom that they enjoy has yet to be won for the nations of the globe. The Revealed will of the Creator must yet overcome the obliquities and prepossessions of men. Prescience must still be exercised to discover the trend of thought and action, and to see that the history of our generation is glorified ere it be handed on to posterity. Popular beliefs must be pruned, dissected, examined upon their merits, and fiercely assailed if not con_ ducive to our improvement in the life of the world. We must not aspire to defend a partizan cry because it is old, or so entangle ourselves in the meshes of infatuation as to be ashamed to abandon that which we have discovered to be wrong. If the Liberation Society declines to discuss the belief in its own Infallibility it must be stormed with all the concomitances*of human scorn. If it still refuses to justify its effort to wreck the principle that has produced a noble nation's character, it must be arraigned as the greatest enemy that England has yet had to meet in the world. If Disestablishers have been cajoled into the advocacy of an attack upon the safeguard of their country's integrity they must nevertheless be treated as adversaries to the highest interests of their land. For five hundred years England has won nearly four-fifths of the battles in which she has been engaged. What would have been the proportion of her victories had she not inscribed the Com- mandments upon her children's lives by the union of Church and State? Were Cressy and Poictiers, Agincort and Blen- heim, Ouenarde and Malplaguet, Trafalgar and Waterloo,

Quebec and Plassy, Alma and Inkerman, Atbara and Omdurman but the pawns in a game of chance, the tossed off sport of fortune, the playthings of a Destiny that was not concerned with the future history of the world! Have not each of these battles paved the way for the enlargement of the British Empire and for the expansion of the character that was first produced by the Union of the English Church and State? Are not each of these victories more attached to our age than to the ages of the men who achieved them for their country? Is not one fourth of the earth's surface already secured to the British race, and has it been bequeathed to us for any other purpose than that of being influenced by the Christianity of the parent State? Were the eighty four per cent. of English victories given to our forefathers for any other object than this? Were those victories intended to be less barren of result than the conquests of Titus and the dispersion of the Jews, or less destined to act as Images for the submersion of the trend of thought? If the acquisition of so much power is but a move in a game of chance can we be certain of maintaining our national greatness for a single day? These are questions that must either be answered by ourselves or by our children. We must either rise to a perception of the potentialities of the connection between a English Church and State or sink to witness the beginning of the end of our country's greatness. The influence of environment is not affected by any accretions that may have been foisted upon the Church for the purpose of circumscribing its comprehensive character. Brave men never shrink from meeting dangers boldly and well. If modern accretions have attempted to obscure the Doctrines of the English Church they must be removed even though at the cost of a Revolution and a civil war. Reforms can only be secured when preceded by upheavals in the courses of human history. Only a coward will think of Disestablishing the Church because it happens to have got into the temporary custody of its enemies. If the Church is Scriptural in theory she must be made Scriptural in practice too. The policies of the State must be the amplification of the thirty nine Articles of Religion so that the lives of Englishmen may be made pliable to the higher standard of personal religious appeal. The character of the subjects of England will become the pattern of the character of the subjects of the Empire and will assist or retard the rehabilitation of Divine decree in the creation of the social powers of the world. As the Christianity of England must of necessity have a paramount influence upon that of the British Empire, so must that of the Empire have a supreme prepossession upon the character of the peoples of the globe. For such a purpose was the British Empire called into being, for the development of Divine intention was it requisitioned to wear the mantles of the mighty Empires of a noble past. The Infantile days of the British Empire will be over when the virgin soil of the earth shall have been occupied and brought under civilized dominion. Each decade is a land-mark in our national destiny, a beating of the pulse of our Empire's life. The next half century will either seal its doom or refurbish its potentialities for the accomplishment of the propagation of Christianity throughout the countries of the Globe. No country save Britain has raised itself to a true appreciation of the value of the Christian faith and of the means that the Creator has provided for incorporating it into the lives of free men. And no Churches save those of England and Scotland have so well perceived that all images of material power were destined to assist in the presentation of the Faith to the minds of created human beings. The Reformers' perception has transcended its own majesty and has produced the grandest moral agency in the British Empire that the world has ever seen. The influence of that Empire must—from the character of its foundation—advance or recede according to the movement of religious sensibility in the parent State and of its efforts to intertwine

itself into the development of moral tone. Living Englishmen have been led on by the trend of events either to make
or to mar an influence that will unostentatiously change the
history of the world. We can only forget that prescience is
the keynote of comprehension at the cost of ruining the
heritage of our children. We cannot shirk our responsibilities or refuse to see that we live in a momentous age.
We must clear the chasm that divides the centuries into
four equal parts or be drawn into the vortex that swallowed
up the Empires of the ancient world. Time awaits the
impress of our decrees but will not allow its patience to be
tried for long. The images of material power were created
for a purpose and will not be allowed to be used by men
whose visions are circumscribed by the age in which they
live. A noble past must be the mentor of a nobler future
whose destiny must be discerned by glancing across the
domains of Time and perceiving why they were carved as
mathematical precisions of Eternity. The potentialities of
the Union between the English Church and State were
intended by the Creator to be too ubiquitous for the
pusillanimous comprehensions of fanaticism on the one hand
or of political flightiness and volatility on the other. The
question is both the kernel of the British Empire's destiny
and the trysting place of the world's career. The freedom
of the human will demands that prescience shall and must
be employed for the discovery of the causes that have produced the Revolutions of history. Disestablishment may
succeed in changing the character of Englishmen by the
substitution of a secular for a Christian environment but
it will not prevent the British Empire from being wrested
from their care. Faithlessness may conceal the elements of
Retribution but only until the time shall be ripe for their
distribution amongst the peoples who have run foul to the
everlasting purposes of God. Men and Empires have their
day and pass on but the thunders of their tread were intended
to resound as the warning voices of history for ever. Ob-

scure are the influences that overshadow the streams of human tendency, unperceived the trivialities that distribute the doctrines of political power. As other Empires have been weighed in the balances and have been found wanting so is England about to be weighed in Eternity's scales. Memorial shadows flit around her burning thoughts each film of light being a precept that cannot die. Voices chant Requiems in the caverns of the mighty dead to rehabilitate the Imageries of living power with the reiterated promise that Righteousness alone shall continue to exalt a nation.

THE END

LAMPETER :

PRINTED BY THE WELSH CHURCH PRESS AND PRINTING CO., LTD.